A CAR FOR ME

A CAR FOR
MR BRADLEY

James Pattinson

CHIVERS LARGE PRINT
BATH

British Library Cataloguing in Publication data available

This Large Print edition published by Chivers Press, Bath, 2001.
Published by arrangement with Robert Hale Ltd.

U.K. Hardcover ISBN 0 7540 4458 0
U.K. Softcover   ISBN 0 7540 4459 9

Copyright © James Pattinson 1983

Printed and bound in Great Britain by
Redwood Books, Trowbridge, Wiltshire

CHAPTER ONE

PROPOSITION

Skene was in bed with the Mexican girl when Holden walked into the room. Skene was asleep with his head half buried in the pillow and his red hair in a fine tangle, as though it had been out in a gale of wind; he was making a noise that was somewhere between heavy breathing and an outright snore, interspersed now and then by a faint whistle like a fancy kettle coming to the boil.

The girl was lying on her back, but she was wide-awake and she sat up when Holden came in. She grinned at him, giving him a big welcome.

'Buenos dias, Ray.'

'Hello, Rosita,' Holden said. 'Do you think you could wake that bastard up?'

She glanced at Skene, who was lying on his right side with his back towards her.

'He is tired, I think. Perhaps we let him sleep, eh?'

'Perhaps we don't. He and I have things to do.'

She gave him a quick, half-suspicious glance. 'What things?'

'Nothing for you to bother yourself about.'

The assurance failed to satisfy her; he could

see that. She was a plump little thing, young, brown-skinned, with nice firm breasts and eyes as black as tar.

'Maybe you ought to get some clothes on,' Holden suggested.

'Why? You don't like me like this?'

'I like you like that, or any other way. But it's time to get up. You can't lie in bed all day.'

Skene woke then. He gazed at Holden, bleary-eyed, pushing back the tangled hair with his fingers.

'You've got a nerve walking in here just as you please. Don't you knock on doors these days?'

'I knocked,' Holden said. 'You didn't hear, that's all. And if you won't want people to walk in you should lock the door.'

'The lock doesn't work.'

That was the kind of hotel it was, not much better than a doss-house; but it was the best they could afford and they were not going to be able to afford even that for many more days. That was why it was so important not to miss the appointment. It might come to nothing after all but they had to take the chance.

The room was small and dingy, and it had a smell about it, a human odour, sensual, cloying, a trifle repellent. But it did not bother Holden; he was not fastidious. He might once have been but not after knocking around so long with a man like Skene.

2

'You know what time it is?'

'No,' Skene said.

'It's past nine. We have to be there by ten. If we're late he may not wait for us. He may think we're not to be relied on.'

'Okay,' Skene said. The bed creaked as he got out of it and reached for the clothes lying in a crumpled heap on a chair. 'Maybe he won't turn up anyway. I'm not counting on it.'

'We'd better hope he does.'

'If he doesn't we'll have to look for something else. We'll get by.'

Holden watched him stepping into his trousers. Skene had a thick, muscular body covered with freckles. He was twenty-eight years old and as strong as they came. Holden had met him for the first time when the two of them joined a thirty-five-foot yacht as part of the crew. The yacht was sailing from Plymouth to Miami, where a buyer was waiting for it. The job finished when the yacht was handed over to its new owner, but they hung on in Florida, taking things easy and enjoying themselves until the money began to run out. Then they managed to get taken on as deckhands aboard a tramp steamer registered in Liberia and sailing from Jacksonville to Rio de Janeiro. Six months later the ship was in Puerto Paramo, a small port on the east coast of Mexico. They were still there but the ship had gone; they had overstayed their shore leave and the captain had not waited for them;

3

time was no doubt more valuable to him than two seamen who could be replaced without difficulty at the next port of call.

So they were on the beach; which was not too bad while they still had some money; but now there was very little money left and something had to be done about it, because even a hotel as cheap and nasty as this one made a charge for its rooms, and food was not handed out for the asking. The crisis might not have arrived quite so early if it had not been for this girl Rosita whom Skene had picked up; he had spent his own money on her and then had borrowed from Holden until there was no more to borrow. Now they were at the end of the line; now everything depended on what Mr Gomez had to offer—if anything.

*   *   *

It was a little past ten o'clock when they walked into the cantina, which was an establishment not far from the waterfront and in much the same class as the hotel. It was where they had originally encountered Gomez, and it could have been that Gomez was on the lookout for them—or somebody like them— broke and only too ready to make a grab at any job that was offered.

Not that he had actually offered them a job—not then; he had simply bought them a couple of drinks and asked a few questions.

4

But Holden would have made a guess that he already knew quite a bit about them, such as the fact that they were British seamen and were on the beach and pretty light in the pocket. Finally he had asked whether they were looking for a way of earning some easy money, because if so he might be able to help them.

To Holden it sounded more than a little dubious, because when somebody you had never seen before came up and suggested he might put you in the way of picking up some easy money the first thought that came into the head was that there must be something slightly illegal about it. But before he could put in a word Skene was already thanking Mr Gomez for his offer and telling him that they would be very pleased to do any little job of work that had a reasonable price-tag on it.

'The fact is,' Skene said, 'we're in a bit of a fix right now and we're open to offers.'

Mr Gomez smiled faintly. 'That was the impression I already had.' He spoke English competently; which was just as well, since neither Holden nor Skene was at all expert in Spanish, though they could make themselves understood sufficiently well in that language for the basic necessities of life.

'What do we have to do to earn this easy money?' Holden asked; and he on his part was not giving Mr Gomez any thanks, because for one thing he had no liking for the man and for another thing it was perfectly obvious that Gomez was not throwing anything their way out of the goodness of his heart; he was doing it simply because he believed it would be to his own advantage.

But Gomez, asked this direct question, had become cagey and had refused to give any details at that time. 'Tomorrow,' he had told them, 'I will speak with you again. Be here in the morning at ten o'clock and I will tell you what you are required to do.'

'Why not tell us now?'

'Because I have to make certain arrangements. Tomorrow I shall be able to tell you for certain whether or not the job is available.'

'Oh, so it's not certain there'll be anything.'

Mr Gomez had given a cynical kind of smile. 'In this life, my friends, only death is certain.'

He had left them then, and when he had gone they had talked the matter over between themselves.

'I think he's a crook,' Holden said.

Skene grinned. 'Maybe he is. But me, I never look a gift horse in the mouth.'

'He hasn't given us anything yet—except a couple of drinks.'

'Well, give him time, give him time. Tomorrow we'll see what he has to talk about.'

'If he turns up.'

'He will. He wants something.'

Skene had been right about that: when they walked into the cantina Gomez was sitting by himself at a table in a corner of the room waiting for them. He seemed pleased and possibly a shade relieved to see them, so perhaps he had had doubts about whether or not they would keep the appointment.

'Ah,' he said, 'so you decided to come.'

'That's what we agreed to do,' Holden said.

'True. But people do not always do what they agree to do. What will you drink?'

'Beer for me,' Holden said.

Skene said he would have the same. Gomez ordered it and it came, cold and frothy, with condensation misting the glasses. The cantina was not very crowded at that hour; there were a few seamen and a few dark-skinned dockside characters who looked as though they might have been left over from the night before.

'You still wish to earn some easy money?' Gomez inquired.

'Well,' Skene said, 'we haven't either of us come into a fortune since we last saw you, so I guess we do.'

Gomez laughed softly but the laughter failed to reach his eyes. Holden thought of snake's eyes; he was quite sure he did not like the man. But this talk of money; it was a seductive subject in the present circumstances.

Gomez lit a cigar. He was a plump, soft-fleshed man with black hair brushed flat across a greasy-looking scalp, and his nose was large and pitted like a ripe strawberry. His lips were moist and there were some pieces of gold scattered here and there inside his mouth; they gleamed when the lips slid back from his teeth. He had stubby-fingered hands, the nails bitten down almost to the quick, and the kind of clothes he was wearing seemed out of place in that company; they had cost too much. He was probably about forty-five years old and had evidently used those years to advantage; by one means or another, legal or illegal, it looked as though he had done pretty well for himself.

'So,' Holden said, 'what do we have to do to earn this money?'

'You have to drive a car.'

'You're telling us you just want a couple of chauffeurs? Or are you talking about a getaway car? Are we expected to help in a bank raid or something?'

'Oh no, nothing like that. Do I look like a man who would rob banks? All you have to do is take this car and deliver it to a certain person. You do drive, of course?'

'I can drive any car you like to name,' Skene said.

'I can drive too,' Holden said. 'But why do you want two drivers? Is there more than one car?'

Gomez shook his head. 'No, only one. But I think you are both in need of work and I am a generous man. One will be company for the

8

other and you can share the driving. It is a long journey.'

'How long?'

'Twelve hundred kilometres. Maybe more.'

They both stared at him.

'Twelve hundred kilometres!' Holden said. 'Where will that take us?'

Gomez drew smoke from his cigar and puffed it out in an aromatic cloud. 'It will take you,' he said, 'to the United States of America.'

Holden was not sure he quite liked the sound of that; in fact he was dead sure he did not.

'So we have to take this car across the border?'

'Precisely. But that is no trouble. You have British passports all in order for letting you into the States?'

'Yes, we've got passports. We were in Florida not so long ago.'

'So what are you worrying about?'

'Who said I was worrying?'

'You look worried.'

'Do I? Well, maybe I am—a little. Why don't you get a Mexican driver? Why pick on us?'

Gomez frowned slightly. 'I do you a good turn and you start asking questions like that? Some people would be grateful. But if you do not want the job—'

Skene cut in very quickly then: 'Of course

9

we want the job. Don't pay any attention to him, Mr Gomez; he just can't believe anyone would want to help us; he's got a suspicious mind.'

'One would think,' Gomez said, a trifle sulkily, 'that I am asking you to do something unpleasant. But what is unpleasant about a nice car ride for which you are being handsomely rewarded?'

'Let's talk about that,' Holden said. 'How much are you offering us?'

'Does it matter if you do not want the job?'

'We want it,' Skene said.

'You want it, but your friend, it seems, does not.'

'Oh, he wants it too. Don't you, Ray, old pal? Tell Mr Gomez you want it.'

Holden shrugged. 'Okay, I want it. Now what's the pay?'

'One thousand American dollars,' Gomez said.

Skene's mouth fell open.

'Where's the catch?' Holden asked.

'No catch.'

'You mean to say you're offering us nearly a dollar per kilometre? More than a dollar a mile?'

'That is so. Four hundred dollars now and the rest when the car is delivered.'

'It's a lot of money for a simple job.'

'I wish to be sure the car is delivered safely.'

'And you think we might be tempted to sell

10

it and pocket the proceeds if the fee is too low? Is that it?'

'Oh, no, no,' Gomez protested. 'I trust you completely. I am quite certain you are both honest men.' Which might have sounded rather more convincing if he had not added: 'And, besides, it would not be good for your health if you pulled a trick like that. Do you understand my meaning?'

Holden understood very well that Gomez was making a threat; and he looked the kind of man who might take some fairly unpleasant measures against anyone who tried to cheat him. So maybe it would be advisable not to.

Skene probably had the same idea, for he said quickly:

'You don't have to worry about that, Mr Gomez. We'll deliver your car all safe and sound, never fear. Who would we sell it to, anyway? We don't know any bent car-dealers in this part of the world.'

Holden thought it might have been better if Skene had not added that last bit; to a suspicious man it could have given the impression that if they had known any bent dealers they might have been tempted. Perhaps Gomez thought so too; he gave Skene a hard look and said:

'I am glad to hear it.'

'So when do we pick up the car?'

'Tomorrow morning at eleven o'clock you must be outside Navarro's curio-shop in the

Calle Cervantes. You know where that is?'

'We know,' Holden said.

'Good. And do not be late.'

Skene promised they would be there on time.

'Who do we take the car to?' Holden asked.

'You will drive to a place in Texas, a small town named Briggsville. You will go to the Red Ace garage and ask for Mr Bradley.'

'So the car is for this Mr Bradley?'

'Yes. You will cross the border at Laredo. There will be a road map in the car, so you should have no trouble in finding the way. The route passes through Mexico City and Monterrey.'

'That's where it happened a long time ago, isn't it?' Skene said, grinning.

'Where what happened?' Gomez asked.

'I forget. Some bloke fell in love with some Judy, I'd say. It was a song; it's what they all do in songs, ain't it?'

'We are not talking about songs,' Gomez said; and he did not sound pleased. It was a serious business and he expected it to be taken seriously.

'You don't think there'll be any bother with the American customs officials at Laredo?' Holden asked.

'Why should there be trouble? You can say you have been on holiday in Mexico and that you thought it would be nice to spend a few days in the States. So you hired the car for the

12

trip.'

'Why don't we tell them the truth?'

'No, no,' Gomez said hastily. 'That would not be advisable. Not at all advisable.'

There surely was something screwy about it, Holden thought. Maybe the car was stolen. Maybe Mr Bradley at the Red Ace garage would do a quick ringing job on it and dispose of it to a Texan customer. It seemed unlikely but unlikely things did happen. In spite of the lure of one thousand dollars he was still far from sure that he wished to be involved. But what alternative was there when you were on your beam-ends in a foreign country? You had to take whatever came along.

Gomez was watching him. 'You do not appear to be entirely happy, Mr Holden. Surely you do not imagine there is anything illegal in this matter?'

'Are you telling me there isn't?' Holden asked.

'But of course I am. All is perfectly legal. You have my word on that.'

For what it was worth, Holden thought. And frankly he would not have wagered a bent halfpenny on the truth of Señor Gomez's word.

But once again Skene chipped in. 'So it's settled then. And if it's all the same to you we'd like the four hundred dollars now, because we're rather pressed for cash and there are a few things we'll need to buy before

13

we leave. Maybe you'd better let us have some of it in pesos. Okay?'

Gomez made no fuss about it. He had apparently come well prepared in the money line and he handed over the dollars and pesos without more ado.

'I suppose we can rely on Mr Bradley to give us the other six hundred when we deliver the car?' Holden said.

'You need have no fear about that,' Gomez assured him. 'Once you have carried out your part of the agreement the money will be yours.'

He seemed to be impatient to break up the party then. He stood up and prepared to leave. His last words before he departed were a final admonition.

'Do not be late tomorrow and do not try any funny business. It would not be to your advantage.'

When he had gone Holden said: 'Did you get the impression that he was threatening us with something nasty if we don't play it straight?'

'Maybe he was,' Skene said. 'But it makes no odds. We're going to play it straight, ain't we?'

'I wasn't proposing to do anything else. I just don't like being threatened, that's all.'

'Forget it, pal. We've got the money, haven't we? And more to come.'

'If everything works out.'

14

'It will.'

Holden drank some beer and looked at Skene. 'What are you going to do about Rosita?'

'How do you mean?' Skene asked.

'Well, she's not going to take kindly to you walking out on her. Not if I'm any judge of character.'

Skene appeared unbothered. 'It's all the same whether she takes kindly to it or not. She'll just have to grin and bear it.'

'She may bear it, but I can't quite see her doing much grinning. Something more in the kicking and screaming line, I'd say.'

'Well, too bad.'

'When will you tell her?'

'I'll tell her tonight,' Skene said. 'I'll tell her we're moving out in the morning and she'll have to find other accommodation.'

'Just like that?'

'Just like that.'

'Well, sooner you than me,' Holden said.

CHAPTER TWO

A Good Used Car

Holden had been dead right about the Mexican girl: she took the news of their imminent departure very unkindly indeed. In

15

fact she made one hell of a fuss about it. Not that she was bothered about Holden's leaving; he could have gone any time he wished and she would not have given a damn. But Skene was a different matter altogether; it seemed she had come to regard him as her man. Maybe she was even in love with him. Holden found that hard to believe but of course he was not Rosita and perhaps Harry Skene looked a far more attractive person from where she was standing.

'You cannot leave me,' Rosita said. 'No, you cannot do it. It is not possible.'

'I can't do anything else, Rosie darling,' Skene told her. 'But maybe it won't be so bad. Maybe I'll be back before long.'

It sounded horribly unconvincing and she was not taken in for a moment.

'Don't tell me lies, you pig,' she said. 'Once you are away from here you never come back. I know. You take this car to the United States and I never see you again, never.'

'Well, it wouldn't be the end of the world, sweetheart.'

'Not the end of the world, oh, no! Not for you, it wouldn't. I see what it is—you don't love me, yes? It is all lies you tell me. You never love me.'

'Of course I love you,' Skene said; and he tried to kiss her but she spat in his face before he could get near enough.

It was hardly ladylike, Holden thought; but

maybe she was no lady and maybe she had some reason for not acting like one. She was working herself up into quite a passion and he would not have been surprised to see her start clawing at Skene with her fingernails.

Skene took out a handkerchief' and wiped his face. 'No, look,' he said, 'there's no point in making all this fuss about it. We have to earn some dollars and, if the way to do it is to drive a car north across the border, that's the way it has to be. You must see that.'

'You do not have to leave me,' she said.

'Well, for Pete's sake! How can I help drive a car to the States without leaving you?'

'You can take me with you, that is how.'

Holden put a word in then; he was afraid Skene might give in to her if she did a bit of wheedling and he wanted to nip that idea right in the bud. There was no way they were going to take a passenger in Mr Bradley's car, and least of all this one; that would simply be asking for trouble. There might well be trouble anyway but there was no sense in letting it step right into the car with you in the shape of little Señorita Rosita Gonzalez, beautiful as that shape might be.

'No,' he said, 'no, no, no! That is something we surely can not do. Not under any circumstances. So you can put that idea clean out of your pretty little head, because it's simply not on.'

She turned the pretty little head and looked

at him; and her eyes seemed to be aflame with anger and to be sending a few sparks in his direction. This time he was afraid she might start clawing at his face and he got ready to defend himself, even if it meant giving her a smart right hook to the jaw; but she made no move towards him.

'You stay out of this,' she said. 'It's none of your damn business.'

'It is my business,' Holden said. 'Harry and I are partners in this thing—fifty-fifty. And there just isn't any room for a third party.'

She looked at Skene. 'Is that what you think, too? Do you say there is no room for me?'

'Well, you see the way it is.' Skene appeared slightly embarrassed. Perhaps he was not finding it quite as easy to discard the girl as he had expected it would be. He hauled a wad of pesos out of his pocket and offered it to her. 'Look, Rosie, here's some money to keep you going. You'll be okay.'

She scarcely glanced at the wad and made no move to take it. Holden was surprised; he would have expected her to grab what she could get; but maybe she was not as mercenary as he had imagined.

'So now,' she said, 'I'm supposed to take a few filthy pesos and just fade away? You have had all you want from me and now you are paying me off. Big deal!'

'You've got it all wrong,' Skene said. 'It's not

18

like that; it's a present.' He took a step towards her, holding out the bundle of notes. 'Take it.'

She knocked his hand aside with an angry gesture. 'I don't want your lousy money; you can keep it. I want none of it.'

'You should take it while you have the chance,' Holden said. 'Money is always useful. It's what pays the bills, you know.'

'Why don't you go away?' she said. 'This is between me and Harry.'

'Maybe so, but I have an interest in it. It concerns me too.'

'All the same,' Skene said, 'it might be best if you left us to work it out between ourselves.'

Holden hesitated. He had a feeling that if he left them to it Rosita might persuade Skene to change his mind about leaving her; a girl like that could bring a lot of pressure to bear, and Skene was susceptible to her charms, that was certain. She had a lot going for her, one way and another.

'Well,' he said, 'just so long as it's understood that whatever happens she doesn't come with us, all right. But there's no way we're going to have three in that car, no way at all.'

'Don't worry yourself about that,' Skene said. 'It's going to be okay.'

The girl said nothing but she had begun to weep, not making a sound but just letting the tears ooze out of those large dark eyes and trickle down her cheeks.

'Now, Rosie sweetheart,' Skene said coaxingly, 'there's no need to cry. Everything will be all right.'

Holden walked out of the room and left them to sort it out as best they could.

He went to a nearby bar and ordered a beer. There were some American seamen in there and they were half drunk and being noisy. He steered clear of them and made his drink a slow one as he wondered how things were going between Skene and Rosita. He had been pally with Skene for nearly a year now but he still did not entirely understand the man and sometimes he was not even sure he liked him. Skene could be very moody at times and he had a foul temper when roused. There was certainly a mean streak in him, but Holden told himself that you had to make allowances for someone who had been, quite literally, found on a rubbish dump and had never known his parents.

Holden himself had had a very different kind of upbringing; he had had a comfortable middle-class home, a good education, every advantage. Yet most people would probably have said that he had wilfully thrown away his chances. If he had wished he might have gone into the legal profession like his father, who was a solicitor in a small country town; but it had not appealed to him. Instead he had chosen to lead a vagrant sort of life, picking up a precarious living by one means and another.

Now, at the age of twenty-six, he had little enough to show for his activities—no money, no steady employment, no future to speak of. He had a load of experience but it was hardly a marketable commodity, and there were times when he asked himself just where he was going, what it was all leading to. Had he after all chosen the right path? For it surely was true what the old saw said about a rolling stone gathering no moss, and he had never heard of anyone making his fortune by taking the odd driving job for men like Mr Gomez. And when you came to think about it 'odd' was probably the right adjective.

One of the American seamen glanced in his direction and said: 'Hi feller, why don't you come along over and join the party? No fun drinking on your ownsome.'

'Thanks,' Holden said, 'but I have to leave now. I have an appointment.'

He finished his beer and went back to the hotel.

Skene seemed to have ironed things out with Rosita. She was not crying any longer and she looked happy. Holden glanced at Skene, faintly suspicious.

'Well?'

'Well what?' Skene said.

'You came to an agreement?'

'Oh, sure. Rosie's an intelligent girl. I just explained to her that you can't always have things exactly the way you'd like; that isn't the

21

way the world goes round. Something has to give.'

Holden turned his eyes on the girl. 'And you gave?'

She grinned at him; all her anger against him had apparently evaporated. 'Yes, Ray, I give. Always I give. Me, I am one generous girl.'

'And you're quite happy now?'

'Oh, yes. It will not be for long. Soon Harry and me, we are together again and all is good.'

So he had managed to convince her that he would be coming back. Well, maybe he would, though Holden doubted it. He himself had no intention of returning to Mexico. Once he had the balance of the dollars in his hands he would move on; there ought to be something a man with ability could pick up in the United States. And he had a feeling that Skene would go with him. He felt a slight prick of conscience when he looked at the girl, starry-eyed, believing Skene's promises. She could be in for a big disappointment. But it was not his fault; he was not the one who was abandoning her.

'So all is good,' he said. 'Fine.'

He looked at Skene, and Skene gave a wink which seemed to confirm his suspicion that the girl was being conned and that there would be no happy reunion. For a moment he almost hated the other man and felt an inclination to tell Rosita not to believe a word she had been

22

told; but what good would it have done? Maybe she would have preferred to accept Skene's word anyway, and there would just have been a lot more argument to no purpose. Better to leave things as they were.

'And now,' Skene said, 'I think we should all go out and enjoy ourselves. Tomorrow we have to start working for a living.'

*   *   *

There was no sign of the girl when Holden went to Skene's room in the morning. None of her clothes were lying around, either.

'Where's Rosita?' he asked.

'Gone,' Skene said.

'She must have left early.'

'She did.'

'Where's she gone?'

'How would I know? She didn't tell me.'

'And you didn't ask?'

'No.'

It seemed a bit odd to Holden. 'How does she expect you to get in touch with her when you come back?'

Skene gave a grin. 'Now that,' he said, 'is something that just never occurred to me.'

'You don't intend coming back, do you?'

'Oh, I don't know. We'll see how it goes.'

'She's expecting you to. She trusts you; she doesn't think you'd lie to her.'

'That's true. You wouldn't think anyone

23

would be so trusting in this bad old world, would you?'

'I'll tell you something, Harry,' Holden said. 'I think you're a bit of a bastard.'

Skene just laughed.

*   *   *

They were at the appointed rendezvous well before eleven o'clock. They were carrying what little personal gear they had in a couple of plastic zipper-bags and as they waited Holden had time to reflect that the bags held just about all they possessed; which was not much to show when you were getting well into your late twenties.

The Calle Cervantes was an ancient narrow street through which quite a lot of traffic of various kinds was flowing. Navarro's curio-shop would not have been difficult to find even if they had not already known where it was; the name was spelt out in big red lettering above the entrance and the windows were full of the kind of junk that people bought as souvenirs to prove how far away they had been from their own backyards. A little black-haired man with a big moustache and sideboards, who might have been Navarro in person, came out and tried to entice Holden and Skene to step inside. It was not easy to convince him that they were not in the market for any of his merchandise but they managed it in the end

24

and he went back inside, a disappointed man.

'I don't see Gomez's car,' Skene said.

Holden looked at his watch. 'It's not eleven yet.'

'I just hope he's not going to let us down after all.'

Skene sounded a trifle anxious, which rather surprised Holden. He had been the one who was so sure they could trust Gomez.

'Why should he let us down? He's paid us four hundred dollars and there's a job he wants done. He's not likely to throw good money away for the fun of it.'

'Maybe you're right,' Skene said. 'But I hope he's not going to be late.'

Eleven o'clock came but no Mr Gomez. At a quarter past eleven there was still no car and Holden was beginning to share Skene's anxiety. He was uneasily conscious of the presence of the little black-haired man, who had reappeared in the doorway of the shop and was regarding them with a certain curiosity. Perhaps they were making themselves conspicuous waiting with their plastic bags at what was certainly not a bus-stop; and to be conspicuous was not what Holden would have wanted.

'What in hell's keeping him?' Skene said. 'He should have been here by now.'

'Maybe he had an accident.'

'An accident! That'd be just fine, wouldn't it? An accident before we've even started. An accident! Jeeze!'

'Calm down,' Holden said. 'It was only a thought. Probably nothing's happened except he overslept or something.'

'So that's the kind of joker we're dealing with—a guy who oversleeps when he's got an appointment to keep. You'd think he could afford an alarm-clock.'

'We don't know he overslept. It was only a suggestion.'

'We don't know anything,' Skene grumbled. 'Maybe we oughtn't never to have taken the damn job.'

'You were the one who was so keen on it.'

'So now you're blaming me? It's all my fault, is it?'

'I'm not blaming anyone,' Holden said.

And at that moment he saw the blonde.

The blonde had long straight hair the colour of bleached straw. She was wearing sun-glasses with white frames and she was driving a blue Chrysler convertible with the top down. Holden was surprised when she pulled the car to a halt by the kerb just where he and Skene were standing; but he was even more surprised when she looked towards them and said in a clear, cool voice:

'You two boys wouldn't be waiting for a lift by any chance, would you?'

There was a certain huskiness in the voice and she spoke with an American accent. Holden made a rough guess and put her age at

26

not more than twenty-five, which was a pretty good age for a blonde to be. There was no need to make any guesses about her physical attributes; it was easy to see she had plenty.

'Thanks,' Holden, said. 'It's a nice offer—if it was meant to be an offer—but we're waiting for a bus.'

The blonde gave a laugh. 'I think you just got it.' She opened the door and stepped out of the car. She was wearing faded jeans and a check shirt and she was taller than average. 'Mr Holden and Mr Skene?' she said; but the question was a mere formality.

'That's us.' Holden said.

'Mr Gomez said you'd be here. I'm Marcia Brent.'

'Pleased to meet you, Miss Brent,' Skene said; and it sounded as though he meant it. She was the kind of person he would always have been pleased to meet.

'It's hail and farewell,' Miss Brent said. She waved a hand towards the Chrysler. 'It's all yours from here. I guess you have your instructions?'

'You mean you don't come with the car?' Skene said, joking.

She shook her head, throwing the straw-coloured hair into a brief whirl like a ballet-dancer's skirt. 'Sorry. I have other things to do. You'll find the maps and things in the car. Okay?'

'Okay,' Holden said. 'Maybe we'll be seeing

you again sometime.'

Miss Brent gazed at him with candid blue eyes. 'It might be nice at that. But I doubt it.'

Holden doubted it too. He had no idea in what kind of relationship the girl stood to Mr Gomez, but in this matter she was obviously just doing a job. He thought of asking her if she knew why the car had to be delivered to Mr Bradley but decided not to; even if she knew it was not likely she would be telling.

'We'll be on our way, then.' He slung his bag on to the back seat and turned to Skene. 'Do you want me to take first trick at the wheel?'

'No,' Skene said, 'I'll take it. I like driving.' He put his bag with Holden's, got into the driving-seat and had a look at the controls.

Holden thought he seemed very keen to do the first stint; perhaps a little too keen. But maybe it was as he had said, simply because he enjoyed driving. He had certainly not had the chance to do any very recently.

'It's automatic transmission,' Miss Brent said. 'You won't have any trouble. It's as easy to handle as a baby-carriage.'

Holden hoped she was right about the trouble. He got in beside Skene and closed the door. Skene got the car away smoothly enough and slotted it into the traffic. Holden glanced back and saw the blonde and beautiful Marcia Brent standing on the pavement, watching. He gave a wave of the hand but she did not wave back; she turned and walked away in the opposite direction. Somehow he had the impression that she was not sorry to be rid of the car. But he might have been wrong.

The blue Chrysler was in good condition but it was by no means a new car and as far as Holden could see there was nothing out of the ordinary about it. It was just a good used car. Which made it all the more difficult to understand why the mysterious Mr Bradley should want it. But perhaps the car belonged to him; perhaps he had driven it down into Mexico, had had some mechanical trouble with it, had left it with Gomez to be repaired and had returned home by other means. Now the car was in order again and Gomez was sending it back to him. A simple explanation but not one that seemed terribly probable; because if that had been the way of things why had not Gomez told them? And why fork out a thousand dollars for the delivery job?

'I'm still not at all sure I like it,' he said.

Skene was piloting the car with considerable skill through the traffic-congested streets of the old town. He had been living there long enough to become familiar with the layout of the place and he knew the way he had to go in order to get on to the right road.

'You worry too much,' he said.

He himself appeared to be quite happy again now that they were on their way. He obviously did not share Holden's misgivings; his only worry had been that there might be no

29

car.

Puerto Paramo was not a large town and before long they were out on the fringes on the opposite side from the Pacific Ocean where it degenerated into a blight of shanty dwellings, advertising hoardings, rubbish dumps, patches of barren ground and here and there a rusting old car with no wheels and kids playing in it.

'Nice place to live,' Holden said.

Skene just grunted.

A little while later he steered the car to the side of the road and pulled it to a halt.

'What's up?' Holden asked. 'Are you tired of driving already? Do you want me to take over?'

'No,' Skene said.

'So why the stop?'

'Thought you might like to admire the view.'

A white Citroën came up from behind. There were two men in it. The one who was not driving turned his head and looked at the Chrysler. He was not unlike Mr Gomez in appearance but his face was a trifle thinner and darker. The Citroën went past without slackening speed and disappeared round a bend in the road.

'You're crazy,' Holden said.

It was some view. A short way ahead on the right was a single-storey building with a big Coca-Cola sign stuck up outside. There was a vehicle park in front of it with a couple of lorries standing on the sun-baked earth. It was

30

so hot you could see the air shimmering.

Skene sounded the horn three times as if he were giving a signal, and a few seconds later a girl came out of the building. She had a duffle-bag slung over one shoulder, and as soon as she spotted the Chrysler she started running towards it.

'Oh, no!' Holden said.

The girl with the duffle-bag was Rosita Gonzalez.

CHAPTER THREE

LIKE A DEAD MAN

'Oh, yes,' Skene said.

'So this is how you worked it out with her, you scheming bastard. No wonder she went quietly.'

'It saved a lot of argument.'

'Maybe it did. But she's not coming with us. No way is she getting into this car.'

'That isn't what she thinks,' Skene said.

Rosita Gonzalez came up to the car and smiled at them. She was wearing a pale blue shirt and cotton slacks and sandals.

'Hello, Ray,' she said.

'What are you doing here?' Holden asked.

'Waiting for you and Harry. I came out by bus. Do I ride in the back?'

31

'You don't ride in the back or the front. No matter what he may have told you, you're not coming with us. Do you understand?'

He might as well have saved his breath; she appeared not to be listening.

'Nice car,' she said.

'Did you hear what I told you?' Holden asked.

But already Skene had opened the door for her and she was getting into the back, dumping her duffle-bag with the other luggage. Skene got in again behind the wheel.

'No point in making a fuss about it, Ray. What harm can it do to take her along with us? She's nice company.'

He put the car in motion and there was nothing Holden could do but accept the situation.

'You're not mad at me, are you?' Rosita said. 'I promise I won't be any bother.'

'Oh, fine,' Holden said. 'Now I don't have a thing to worry about.'

'Don't be sore,' Skene said. 'It isn't the end of the world if she tags along.'

'Well, I hope you told her it will only be as far as the border.'

'No, I didn't tell her that. I don't see any reason why she shouldn't come all the way if she wants to.'

'I'll give you one good reason—because they won't let her into the States, not without a passport.'

'Now what makes you think she hasn't got one?'

'Well, has she?'

'Sure, she has. She's been to the U.S. before. She lived there for a time.'

Holden turned his head and looked at the girl. 'Is that so?'

'Oh, yes,' she said. 'It is so.'

'Tell him how it happened,' Skene said.

She cast an inquiring glance at Holden. 'Do you want to know?'

'I think maybe you'd better tell me,' Holden said.

So she told him.

'There is this rich American, see? He is in Mexico a while ago, just mooning around on his ownsome. He take a liking to me and ask me to go back home with him to his ranch in Texas. So I have to get a passport, don't I? I mean he is not marrying me or anything like that; I am just going as a friend, a very dear friend.'

'It wouldn't have occurred to you to refuse the invitation, I suppose?'

'Now why would I do that when he has all this lovely money? A million dollars, easy.'

'I can see that must have been a pretty strong argument in favour of accepting. So you went to live with him on his ranch?'

'Yes. It is a most lovely place. I go riding and swimming and tennis-playing, though I am not good at tennis, I am all the time missing

33

the ball or hitting it out; but Joe, he don't mind, he just laugh.'

'It sounds great. Why did you leave?'

'His wife come back and he throw me out. She is the reason he is in Mexico, trying to forget. When they patch things up and come together again there is no more room for me. So I have to go.'

Holden wondered why a girl like Rosita, who could pick up rich Americans, had ever bothered with somebody like Harry Skene, who had scarcely two centavos to rub together and was no Adonis whichever way you looked at him. It just proved that when it came to matters of the heart women could be as crazy as March hares.

'Well,' he said, 'passport or no passport, you're not going across the border with us.'

She pouted like a small child. 'But Harry, he promise I go with you.'

'He had no right to promise anything of the kind without consulting me.'

'I'm consulting you now,' Skene said.

'And the answer is no.'

'Ah, come off it, Ray. What difference does it make? It's a big car, plenty of room.'

Holden gave a sigh. He could see that whatever he said the girl was going to be with them when they crossed the border. And, after all, did it really matter? What she did after they had delivered the car was Harry's problem, not his.

'Okay,' he said, resigned to the situation. 'I can see you mean to take her along, no matter what, so I suppose I may as well withdraw my objection.'

Rosita clapped her hands. She stood up, flung her arms round his neck and kissed him on the cheek. 'You're sweet, Ray. You know that? You're really sweet.'

'Don't slobber over, me,' Holden said. 'I'm not sweet; I'm just weak-willed. I'll probably live to regret this decision.'

She released him and sat down again. She was not bothered about any regrets the future might hold for him; she was just happy to have joined the party. She was the kind of girl who probably never looked more than one step ahead, or maybe two at the most.

A few moments later Holden saw the white Citroën that had passed them when they stopped to pick up Rosita. It was halted by the side of the road and the two men were just sitting in it, doing nothing. It seemed odd to Holden, because they were well clear of the town and there was nothing whatever as far as he could see that anyone would want to stop for at a place like this. For no reason that he could have put his finger on he felt a touch of uneasiness, but he said nothing to Skene.

Both men in the Citroën looked at the Chrysler as it went past. Holden treated them to a hard stare in return but their faces were expressionless and after one fleeting glimpse they were gone.

The road began to climb as they left the coast behind. Skene was driving the Chrysler at a moderate speed, not pushing it at all. Holden approved of this; Gomez had said nothing about getting the car to Mr Bradley within any particular time-limit, so there was no point in doing anything reckless; the object was to get it safely to its destination and collect the dollars, nothing else.

After a while he glanced back along the road, half expecting to see the white Citroën following, but there was no sign of it. Not that he could see very far, since the road twisted one way and then the other as it probed into the foothills of the Sierra Madre del Sur; but anyway there was no good reason to suppose the men in the Citroën would wish to get on their tail; it was just an odd feeling he had that they might.

From a scenic point of view there was much to be said for the car ride they were taking; it was all quite magnificent. That was if you liked mountains. Holden was not sure he did; at least not when you had to drive a car through them to get to your destination and the road might with advantage have been a trifle wider and a good deal better maintained. One could only suppose that the traffic coming up from Puerto Paramo was not heavy enough to warrant money being spent on any improvements. Maybe most of it went by a different route.

If the map could be trusted the road they were following should eventually come to a place called Oaxaca, which according to what Gomez had told them was an old Aztec town, and from there they would be able to get on to the road to Mexico City. Holden just hoped it would be better than this one, because by then it would be his turn to drive. And then he looked back and saw that the white Citroën had come into sight again.

'There's a car just behind,' he said.

'I know,' Skene said. No doubt he had seen it in the driving-mirror.

'I think we're being tailed.'

Skene gave a laugh. 'What gives you that idea?'

'It's the car that passed us just outside Puerto Paramo when we stopped to pick up Rosita, a white Citroën with two men in it. They were parked by the side of the road a bit further on, waiting for us to come up. Now they're on our tail again. At least that's what I think.'

'Are you sure it's the same car?'

'I'm sure.'

'It doesn't prove anything.'

'Maybe not, but I don't like the look of it.'

'Why would anyone want to follow us?'

'I don't know. Because of this car perhaps.'

'How do you mean—because of this car?'

'I mean there's something screwy about the

whole damned business; we could have got ourselves into something that's not going to do either of us a lot of good.'

'So you think those men in the car behind us are police?'

'They could be, but I doubt it. My guess is they're as crooked as I think Gomez is and probably as dangerous as rattlesnakes.'

'Ah, you're imagining things,' Skene said. 'Just because they're behind us doesn't necessarily mean they're doing a tailing job. They happen to be going the same way as we are, that's all.'

But he sounded none too certain all the same. He had his doubts too, that was obvious.

'There's one way of finding out,' Holden said.

'How would that be?'

'Slow down and see if they pass.'

Skene did so. He slowed the Chrysler to little more than a walking pace. The Citroën came no closer; it stayed at a distance of about forty yards behind.

'So what do you think now?' Holden asked.

'I think it's time we lost the bastards,' Skene said.

Rosita had become aware that something was wrong. 'Who are those men in that other car?'

'I don't know,' Holden said. 'But at a rough guess I'd say they're no friends of ours.'

Skene pressed his foot on the accelerator

38

and the Chrysler gathered speed. Briefly the gap between it and the following car widened but the driver of the Citroën was quick to react to the challenge and very soon it was back in the old position. Skene forced some more speed out of the Chrysler but the Citroën appeared to be hanging on with no difficulty at all; it was certainly a fast car.

'You're not losing them,' Holden said. 'Maybe you'd better slow down again before you take us off the road.'

It seemed a distinct and unpleasant possibility that Skene would do just that, for it was not the kind of road anyone would have picked for a motor race; the surface was too uneven, there were too many blind corners and on one side there was a steep drop of several hundred feet which could have made any little error of judgement on the part of the driver extremely dangerous and most probably fatal.

Skene must have come to the same conclusion; he slowed to a less hazardous speed and the driver of the Citroën did the same. Holden breathed rather more easily; he was not happy about having the other car on their tail but there was no sense in killing yourself in order to get rid of it.

For about five miles the situation remained unchanged; the distance between the two cars varied slightly from minute to minute but the Citroën never dropped far behind; it could have been a game the men in it were playing with them.

'Damn them,' Skene said. 'What in hell do they want with us?'

'Perhaps,' the girl suggested, 'they mistake you for someone else.'

Holden thought it unlikely; if there was one thing you could be fairly sure of it was that the men in the other car knew very well whom they were following; they were making no mistake.

They came to a village; it was not much of a place—a few wretched houses, people with jet-black hair and copper skin, barefoot children in ragged clothing, some chickens scratching in the dust, starved-looking dogs. It was a mystery to Holden how anyone managed to get a living in such a place. Not that the living appeared to be anything but meagre. There was not even a Coca-Cola sign, which just showed what a poverty-stricken place it was.

Skene stopped the car where there was a kind of stony square which might have been used as a car-park if there had been any cars to use it. Holden turned his head and saw that the white Citroën had pulled up about twenty-five yards further back. Skene got out of the car.

'What are you going to do?' Holden asked.

'I'm going to have a word with those characters back there,' Skene said.

Holden was going to ask him if he thought

40

that was wise, but already he was on his way, walking with that slightly rolling gait of his, head thrust forward to give a not altogether false impression of belligerence.

'I hope he does not go to make trouble,' Rosita said. She sounded a shade nervous, Holden thought. She had known Skene long enough to be aware that he had something of a gift for making trouble.

Skene reached the Citroën and rested one hand on the roof, bending down and looking in through the window on the driver's side. Some of the children came as close as they dared to the Chrysler and stared at it, standing in a tight little group as though to give one another courage. An ancient lorry, packed with wooden crates and coarse sacks and a few human beings perched precariously on the load, went by in a cloud of dust, engine complaining loudly and mudguards rattling. Skene gave a shrug, took his hand off the Citroën and returned to the Chrysler. He got in without a word and slammed the door.

'Well?' Holden asked. 'What did they say?'

'Nothing. Not a damned bloody thing. They just looked at me like I wasn't there; just stared straight through me like I was a ghost.' He paused, as though thinking about it, then added musingly: 'Or maybe like I was a dead man. Yes, that's it, like I was a dead man.'

Holden rather wished he had not said that. The girl seemed unhappy too; perhaps she was beginning to wonder why she had been so keen to join the party.

'Maybe they didn't understand what you were saying,' Holden suggested.

But Skene was having none of it. 'They understood all right, you can bet your sweet life on that. They understood, the bastards. And they just looked at me like I was dead.'

The men had certainly made an impression on him, Holden thought; but it had not been a favourable one.

Skene got the Chrysler moving again and the kids hopped out of the way like a scattering of sparrows. Holden glanced back to check that the Citroën was following. It was. He would have been surprised if it had been otherwise.

Beyond the village the road became even worse than it had been before. Skene kept the Chrysler going at a moderate speed and the Citroën stayed tucked in behind, and this went on for a few more miles with the tyres hammering on the stones and potholes and a lot of impressive mountain scenery rolling past like something out of a travel film. Then suddenly the men in the Citroën appeared to decide that the time had come to start the action. The one who was driving stood on the accelerator and before Skene realised what was happening the white car had closed up with the Chrysler and was no more than half a dozen yards behind.

42

Holden looked over his shoulder and saw what was happening. He shouted a warning to Skene:

'Look out, Harry. I think they're trying to pass.'

'To hell with that,' Skene said and he accelerated too, keeping the Chrysler in the middle of the road. 'If we let the bastards get in front there's no telling what they may do. I think they've got a hijack in mind.'

'You could be right,' Holden said. The men could have been waiting until they reached a predetermined spot before carrying out the operation and now the time had come.

The driver of the Citroën was certainly making great efforts to get past but was being frustrated by Skene's blocking tactics; he was sounding the horn furiously but to no avail. This went on for quite a while and then the man who was not driving seemed to lose patience and decided to resort to more violent methods. Holden saw him lean out of the side window with something gripped in his right hand. And then the something made a sharp cracking sound and he knew that it was a pistol.

'My God, Harry,' he shouted, 'they're shooting at us. Step on it.'

The girl gave a startled yelp and got herself off the rear seat and down on the floor so quickly it was like a stage vanishing act; one moment she was there and the next moment

43

she had gone.

On his part Skene required no urging; a gun firing at him from behind was more than sufficient as a spur and he put his foot down hard on the accelerator. A moment later the man with the pistol got pretty well on target and a bullet zipped through the windscreen, making a small hole and a fairly large area of semi-opacity.

'Bloody hell!' Skene yelled. 'He nearly hit me.'

Just then, as if to make matters worse, a big covered van came round a bend in the road ahead and rumbled towards them, taking up more than its fair share of the available space. Holden caught a glimpse of it bearing down on them and gave a cry of alarm.

'For God's sake, Harry! You're going to hit that lorry.'

It certainly looked like it. Skene was not seeing too well through the shattered windscreen and he must have caught sight of the van at the last moment coming at him like a house on wheels. There was a wall of rock on the right hand side of the road and he tried to squeeze the car between this and the van. The driver of the van was not giving him much room because on the other side of the road was a drop of a few hundred feet and if he took his vehicle over the edge there was no way he was going to come out of it alive.

Skene was cursing and gripping the wheel

like a madman and it looked for one terrible moment as if the Chrysler and the van would collide head-on. Then there was a rending, screeching sound and a hell of a jolt which almost threw Holden out of his seat, then more jolting and jarring and grinding of metal on metal, and a second later they had scraped past and were clear. They had come through in one piece and Holden was dead sure he would never understand just how they had done it. There had not been room; there really had not been room, and yet somehow they had made it. Luck, maybe.

He glanced back to see what was happening to the other car and he was just in time to witness a truly spectacular smash-up. The driver of the Citroën had been so intent on keeping up with the Chrysler that he had either failed to see the van until it was too late or had imagined he could squeeze past it as Skene had done. And he too might have made it if the van had not lurched across to the left just as the Citroën approached at high speed. The driver of the Citroën tried to pull further over to his right and the van hit the car just behind the off-side front wheel, so that it seemed to rebound like a billiard-ball striking a cushion. Under the force of the impact it swivelled even further to the right and slammed full-tilt into the unyielding wall of rock. The van bulldozed its way past, travelled on for a short distance and then came to a halt.

'Stop the car, Harry,' Holden said.

Skene did so.

Rosita's head came into view; she looked scared and her hair was in a mess.

'What happened?'

Neither Skene nor Holden bothered to answer. They got out of the car and walked back along the road. The white Citroën was in pretty bad shape, with the front crushed in as though it had been hit by a tank; but even at that it was in better shape than the men inside it; they had really taken a beating and there was blood all over the place.

'I can tell you something, Ray,' Skene said. 'We don't have to bother ourselves any more about those jokers.'

He sounded amazingly cool, Holden thought. He himself felt sick at the sight of the mangled bodies.

'Another inch or two and we could have been like that.'

'But we aren't. And don't expect me to be sorry for the bastards. They tried to kill us, didn't they? And we never did them any harm.'

Holden heard a kind of strangled gasp. The girl had joined them and was staring wide-eyed at the dead men. Then she turned away and walked a little unsteadily back to the Chrysler.

The van was about thirty yards down the road. The driver got out and came towards them; he was a big fat unshaven man in greasy

46

dungarees and a baseball cap. He looked shocked and he began to talk so fast Holden could not understand a word he was saying. He peered at the bodies in the Citroën and he must have caught sight of the pistol which was still in the hand of the one who had done the shooting. It seemed to make him even more excited; he began waving his arms and yelling at Skene and Holden.

'Let's get out of here,' Skene said.

It sounded like a good suggestion to Holden. Before long there would be some more people arriving on the scene, and maybe the police; and then there would be a lot of difficult explaining to do. He was not at all sure he wanted to try giving an explanation of what had happened there; he just wanted to get away from it all.

They walked back to the Chrysler and the fat van-driver followed them, still gesticulating and talking at a great rate. The girl was already sitting in the car. Skene picked up a lump of rock and knocked the shattered glass out of the windscreen. He and Holden got in. The van-driver gripped the top of the door with his hands and shouted at Skene.

'What the devil is he making so much fuss about?' Skene said. 'He's not the one who got hurt.'

'He say you cannot just drive away and leave him,' Rosita explained. 'He say this is a matter for the police. He say the two men are dead

47

and his lorry is damaged.'

'The hell with his lorry,' Skene said. He started the engine.

The fat man made a grab at Skene as if to prevent him from driving. Skene clenched his right fist and drove it hard into the man's throat. The man staggered back from the car, making choking noises. Skene put the car in gear and got it moving. There was a harsh grinding sound coming from the rear; the wing on the off side had been crumpled in the encounter with the van and was pressing on the wheel.

Skene ignored the racket and drove on. Holden looked back and saw the fat man shaking his fist at them. He wondered whether the man had taken the Chrysler's registration number. It seemed doubtful.

CHAPTER FOUR

A Good Question

'You know something?' Skene said. 'Those two jokers were really out to get us.'

'It seems likely,' Holden admitted. It would hardly have been possible to come to any other conclusion.

'So why?'

'I don't know. Perhaps, like Rosita

suggested, it was a case of mistaken identity. Perhaps they thought we were some other people.'

'Bullshit. They had a good look at us, didn't they?'

'That's true.'

'So how could they've made a mistake?'

'I don't know.'

'If you ask me,' Skene said, after giving it a bit more thought, 'I'd say they wanted something from us.'

'What have we got they would want as badly as all that?'

'Only the car.'

'You think they'd kill us to get the car—and risk smashing it up in the process? It doesn't make much sense to me.'

'Maybe it does make sense at that,' Skene said; but he did not elaborate.

There was still quite a racket coming from the rear wheel where the crumpled metal was pressing on it. It was the kind of thing that, together with the smashed windscreen, was likely to attract unwelcome attention. Holden remarked on it to Skene.

'I've been thinking about that,' Skene said. 'The first chance we get I'm going to take this wagon off the road where we can do some work on it without anyone coming along and asking us what we're up to.'

A few minutes later the opportunity presented itself: a narrow stony track, possibly formed by natural means, led off to the left, curving away between rough walls of rock until it ended abruptly in an oval enclosure completely hidden from the road. In this secluded place Skene stopped the car and switched off the engine. For a while all three of them remained sitting where they were, saying nothing, as though savouring this moment of almost utter stillness and silence. Then Holden said:

'Okay, so how about getting started on that rear wing?'

'Damn the wing,' Skene said.

'But I thought that was what you brought us in here for—to work on it.'

'Maybe you did. But you were wrong, pal. I brought you in here so we could take a real close look at this car we're supposed to deliver to Mr Bradley.'

'Now why do you want to do that?'

'Because,' Skene said, 'a car that's as valuable as this one certainly has to have something very extra special about it, and I mean to find out just what that something is. Get me?'

Holden saw that Skene had a point there. 'I get you.'

They both got out of the car and Rosita followed suit. She seemed pretty bewildered by what was going on, but she was not asking a lot of stupid questions, which was rather surprising in the circumstances.

Skene opened the boot and poked around inside without finding anything of interest.

'It wasn't likely to be in there anyway,' he said.

'What wasn't?' Holden asked.

'What we're looking for.'

'What are we looking for?'

'I don't know,' Skene said. 'But I'll know when I find it.'

After that he really got going on the search and soon the upholstery was in a shocking state. He had used a knife and had done a thorough ripping job; a gang of football fans could not have done a better one on a railway carriage after a cup-tie.

'Mr Bradley isn't going to think much of this when we deliver the car,' Holden said.

Skene made a rude gesture. 'That to Mr bloody Bradley.'

'Señor Gomez may not be very pleased, either.'

'And Señor bloody Gomez,' Skene said, 'can go and take a running jump.'

Then he went to work on the car again.

The girl was still saying nothing; she was sitting on a small boulder, just watching what was going on. She probably thought Skene had gone crazy and she might not have been far wrong at that. The luggage was standing in a little pile on the ground nearby; it would have been in the way if they had left it in the car.

When he had finished ripping out the

51

upholstery Skene had a go at the doors with a tyre-lever and a hammer from the tool-kit. Holden gave him a hand; he had stopped worrying about what Mr Bradley or Mr Gomez would think; it was dead certain they were never going to deliver the car now, anyway; they would just have to be satisfied with the four hundred dollars advance pay and hope to steer clear of any repercussions.

There was nothing hidden in the doors or the wheel arches or behind the dashboard or in a dozen other likely or unlikely places. Skene did some work with his knife on the spare tyre, but there was nothing inside it except a lot of compressed air. Holden had already given up expecting to find anything, and even Skene seemed to be having doubts, though he did not admit it. He stopped work and smoked a cigarette, sitting on the boulder with Rosita and gazing thoughtfully at the badly-used Chrysler which the blonde in Puerto Paramo had handed over to them in almost perfect condition only a short time ago. She would have had a shock if she could have seen what it looked like now.

'I think we ought to be going,' Holden said. He was not at all happy with the situation and had no desire to be found with a car that seemed to have become an incriminating piece of hardware. Not, of course, that anyone was likely to come looking for it where it was at this moment. All the same . . .

'Ah, damn it!' Skene said. He threw the half-smoked cigarette away, walked back to the car and lifted the bonnet.

Holden strolled over and joined him. 'What do you think you're going to find in there?' he asked. 'Besides a few sparking-plugs and this and that.'

'Oh, for God's sake!' Skene said. 'I told you I don't know. But there's got to be something; it stands to reason. There just has to be something and I'm damn well going to find it.'

'There wouldn't be anything in the engine.'

'How do you know? There could be.'

He started poking around with a screwdriver in a haphazard sort of way.

'You want to be careful,' Holden said. 'You could cause a short and maybe start a fire.'

Skene stopped poking. 'Let's have the damned battery out of the way, then. Maybe it's hiding something.'

Holden thought it unlikely but Skene was already disconnecting the leads. It was a big battery; Holden had never seen a bigger one on a car. He had to give Skene some help in lifting it out. But it had not been hiding anything as far as he could see.

They carried it a few yards away from the car and they were still carrying it when Skene stumbled on a piece of rock and the battery slipped from his grasp. Holden let his end go, too, and jumped out of the way to avoid getting a crushed toe. The battery hit the ground fairly hard, and a strange thing happened: the entire lower portion broke away from the top, but no acid spilled out, just half a dozen small polythene bags with something inside them.

'Ah!' Skene said and there was a note of triumph in his voice. 'Now what have we here?'

He picked up one of the bags. It was fastened with a metal clip. He removed the clip and opened the bag. Inside was a white powdery substance.

'You know what this is?' Skene said.

Holden looked at the white substance and hazarded a guess. 'Heroin?'

'I wouldn't be at all surprised, old buddy mine. I wouldn't be at all surprised.'

'That would explain quite a lot.'

'You bet it would.'

Rosita had come to take a closer look. She turned to Skene. 'So you are carrying drugs in the car. You know this, Harry?'

'Now talk sense,' Skene said. 'Of course we didn't know it. We were just being used by that bastard, Gomez. He was getting us to run his drugs across the border. Nice for him; if we get caught he's okay. Maybe it's a regular business; he keeps an eye open for likely drivers to deliver cars to Mr Bradley and what they're really delivering is narcotics. At a thousand dollars a go it's pretty damned cheap.'

'So how about the men in the Citroën? Do you think they were police after all? We're in a nice fix if they were,' Holden said.

'No,' Skene said. 'I'd say they were more likely another set of villains who maybe got wind of the shipment and decided to hijack it. Could have been business rivals of Mr Gomez, possibly somebody he did the dirty on, anything. We were the poor idiots who got caught in the crossfire.'

Holden thought Skene was probably right; in the kind of racket Gomez was apparently engaged in there was bound to be a lot of double-crossing and feuding. And from what he had heard it was a multi-million dollar racket, with the United States law-enforcement officers and customs men picking up only the merest fraction of the narcotics that came over the border in an ever-increasing flood. These half-dozen polythene bags represented no more than a drop in the bucket, and a very small drop at that.

'How much would you reckon this lot is worth on the American market?'

Skene pushed out his lower lip. 'If I was to make a guess it'd likely be a thousand miles wide of the mark. I just don't know. It's a trade I never had anything to do with—until now.'

The way he said 'until now' caused Holden to give him a swift glance. He had a feeling that he could guess what was taking root in Skene's mind, and he was not at all sure he liked it.

Skene turned to the girl. 'I suppose you wouldn't know anything about the value of heroin on the illicit market?'

She shook her head in quick denial. 'I never have any part in drugs, never.'

Holden wondered whether she was telling the truth. Maybe she was a shade too vehement.

'Are you telling us you've never even had a whiff of cannabis, never smoked a reefer?'

'Yes, that is exactly what I am telling you. Why don't you believe me?'

'Who said I didn't believe you?'

'Forget it, Ray,' Skene said. 'It's not important. This here is what's important.' He pointed at the polythene bags lying on the ground at his feet. 'This is cash in the bank for you and me.'

'Now wait a minute,' Holden said. 'Are you suggesting we sell this stuff on our own account?'

'Why not? Can you give me one good cast-iron reason why we shouldn't?'

'I can give you a dozen good reasons. In the first place it doesn't belong to us; we've got no right to handle something that's not ours.'

'The way I look at it,' Skene said, 'we've got plenty of right. You could call it compensation for what's happened to us. Gomez owes us something; he hoodwinked us; he didn't tell us what we might be letting ourselves in for.

56

Damnit all, we might have been killed.'

'I know that. But it doesn't mean we're entitled to take the stuff across the border and put it up for sale. Even if it was ours it wouldn't be legal. As I understand it that sort of thing is strictly against the laws of the United States of America.'

'So what are you suggesting we do? Just walk away and leave a small fortune lying where it is?'

'Maybe we should hand it over to the Mexican police,' Holden said. But he spoke doubtfully; he could not honestly have said that he was in very great favour of the idea himself.

And it brought Rosita into the argument. She said vehemently: 'No, you must not do that. If you go to the police you and Harry are in bad trouble.'

'Why? We've done nothing illegal.'

'No?' Skene said. He glanced at the wrecked car and the polythene bags. 'You really want to try convincing some hard-nosed Mexican coppers that you're innocent of any crime? You really and truly want to do that?'

Holden said nothing. It was not a prospect he found at all entrancing.

Skene grinned. 'Now you're beginning to see things my way, aren't you?'

'I'm trying hard not to,' Holden said. 'Your way could land us up to our necks in trouble—big trouble. And, besides, I don't care for the notion of becoming a drug-runner. There's the moral aspect to consider. It's got a nasty taste to it.'

'Now don't tell me your conscience is bothering you. That'd be a fine thing.'

'Does it seem so unlikely to you?'

'It seems plain foolish to me,' Skene said. 'Look at it this way: nobody has to go on drugs; they do it because they want to; and they'll get the stuff anyway, whatever we do or do not do. So what difference does it make whether or not we take a few bags of heroin over the border and make ourselves a small packet? It's not going to hurt anybody, you know.'

'Harry's right,' the girl said. She was on Skene's side. She would be.

And after all, Holden thought, perhaps he was right. Would it really benefit anyone if they threw away this opportunity of picking up some quick easy money? Not likely.

'What are you going to do with the car?' he asked. 'Leave it here?'

'There's not much choice, is there? The way it is now it'd be a bit conspicuous, even if we could get it going. Which is doubtful.'

In the end they decided to set fire to it; it seemed the surest way of removing any fingerprints. They stowed the polythene bags in their luggage and the car was still burning when they left it and walked back to the road.

They rode into Oaxaca on the back of a

lorry. It cost them ten pesos. There were about a dozen other passengers, some crates of chickens, a few sacks of vegetables, an old refrigerator and a couple of goats already on board, and it would have been about as comfortable riding inside a cement-mixer, but it was easier than walking. If anyone thought it at all strange that two men and a girl with hand luggage should be thumbing a lift in that remote spot they did not remark on it. The driver had a face like an old gardening glove, devoid of expression. He took their money and asked no questions. There were two other men in the cab with him and they asked no questions either; it was none of their business what other people did.

If they had been tourists they might have spent some time looking round Oaxaca, which was a picturesque old town dating back to the time of the Aztecs, before stout Cortez and his conquistadores arrived on the scene to erect the cross on a foundation of blood and destruction. They might have bought pieces of Indian pottery and leatherwork and brightly coloured blankets to take home as souvenirs, and if they had had cameras they might have taken photographs to exhibit to bored friends and relations. They might in fact have done everything that tourists customarily did and had a whale of a time.

But they were not tourists and they had no interest in the history of the town or the artefacts of the people. Their one aim was to get out of there and start on their way north with as little delay as possible.

'From here,' Skene said, 'I suggest we go by train.'

It seemed a good enough idea and they found the railway station without difficulty. They had an hour to wait for the train and as it was a long time since they had last had anything to eat or drink they bought some refreshment. They took great care not to let the zipper-bags out of their sight for an instant, because what was inside them now was worth a lot more than a few items of clothing and toiletry, the devil of a lot more.

Holden was still far from happy with what they were doing but Skene seemed to have no qualms.

'Everything is going to be fine, pal. We're going to be in the money. Just you wait and see.'

Holden's misgivings were not swept away by these reassuring words. He could visualise all kinds of difficulties ahead; getting the heroin across the border was only the start of the business. If they got past that obstacle safely they still had to find a buyer and do a deal. None of it was going to be easy and all of it was likely to be more than a little dangerous.

'We're crazy,' he said. 'It'll never work out.'

'Sure it will,' Skene said. He seemed to have no doubts at all. 'We're the lucky boys, ain't

60

we? It was the other guys that got themselves killed. Somebody up there is on our side.'

'It could be us who get killed next time.'

'Not a chance. You worry too much.'

'With someone like you for a partner I've surely got cause to worry,' Holden said.

Skene laughed.

It was late in the evening when the train rolled into Mexico City. The two Englishmen and the Mexican girl spent the night on the station; it was cheaper than finding hotel accommodation and it had become advisable to be careful with the pesos. Some day they might be rich but for the present their working capital was limited.

For this reason they decided not to travel by train to Laredo but to seek a cheaper form of transport. They made a frugal breakfast and soon after ten o'clock they had the good fortune to be in a Datsun station-wagon being carried effortlessly on their way by a garrulous middle-aged Mexican who appeared to be only too glad to have their company, or at least the company of Rosita, who was sitting beside him on the front seat. It was a bit crowded in the back, since the Mexican had apparently been doing a great deal of shopping, chiefly in the provision line, but neither Holden nor Skene was making any complaint.

The Mexican's name was Carlos Carrera; he was a plump, round-faced man with a black moustache and twinkling eyes. When he laughed—and laughter came easily to him—he revealed a set of big white teeth that looked like a tooth-paste advertisement. He was, so he told them, the proprietor of a transport café about sixty kilometres north of Mexico City; he could take them as far as that but then they would have to find another driver.

'But it will not be difficult. Plenty trucks pull in at my place. Somebody will take you.'

Carrera was bilingual; he spoke Spanish to the girl and switched to English when addressing Holden and Skene. He drove fast and talked all the time, pausing only with reluctance to listen now and then to what they had to say. It was a fine clear day and the sun shone down from an almost cloudless sky but at that alititude the air was fresh and temperate. To the south the snow-capped peaks of the Sierra Nevada were visible, standing whitely against the sky, and the words of a poem he had learnt as a boy came into Holden's mind.

'I stood where Popocatapetl
In the sunlight gleams.'

But which of those peaks gleaming in the sunlight was Popocatapetl and which Ixtaccihuatl? Carrera might possibly have been able to tell him but he did not ask. Better not to distract the Mexican from his driving; there was too much traffic on the highway.

62

'You guys like Mexico?' Carrera asked.

'We like it,' Skene said. 'It's a nice country.'

'So why you want to leave?'

'That's a good question,' Skene said. But he did not answer it.

CHAPTER FIVE

Brunhilde

Carlos Carrera's transport café was a long low building about fifty yards off the highway, with a big tarred forecourt on which a number of articulated lorries were parked. Adjoining it was a filling-station with a row of petrol-pumps and Carrera said that this was his also. He appeared to have a very profitable business.

There were a few other, smaller buildings scattered around and a lot of garish signs inviting custom in Spanish and English. Neither the buildings nor the signs did much for the scenic beauty of the place but Holden doubted whether a little thing like that would bother Señor Carrera; there was no money in the scenery.

He drove the station-wagon round to the back of the café where there were crates of empty bottles, piles of cardboard cartons and a litter of assorted garbage.

'You want to eat?' he asked.

It was getting on for midday and Holden for one was feeling hungry; it was some time since they had had their early and rather meagre breakfast. Besides, they owed it to Carrera to patronise his establishment, since he was not charging them anything for the transport.

'That sounds like a good suggestion,' he said.

Carrera led them in through the kitchen, where a fat woman was busy over a stove and another, slightly less fat, was chopping vegetables on a table. In the part where the customers ate there was a long counter with a reef of stools and some off-shore islands of tables and chairs. The place was about a third full. The clientele was predominantly male and Rosita caused a number of heads to turn but appeared unembarrassed; she was used to having that kind of effect on the opposite sex. Carrera found a vacant table and took their order himself.

'You know anyone here that's going to Laredo?' Skene asked. 'Someone that'd be willing to take us.'

'I will make inquiries,' Carrera promised. 'Be patient. First you eat.'

He left them and disappeared through the doorway to the kitchen by which they had entered. After a while the food was brought to them by a young girl with hair tied in a pony-tail that reached half-way to her waist. She smiled all the time she was serving the meal

64

but said very little.

'I wonder,' Skene said when the girl had gone, 'whether anybody has found the car yet.'

Holden thought it very possible. 'The police are bound to be looking into the death of those men in the Citroën; they'll be hunting for the other car involved and they'll maybe have been using a helicopter.'

'Well, it makes no difference. They don't know who we are.'

'The van-driver will have given our description; that's for certain.'

'And if his descriptions are no better than most people's it won't help them a lot.'

'Two men and a girl—they'll maybe keep a watch at the border.'

'Ah, stop worrying,' Skene said. 'We'll be okay, I betcher.'

They had finished eating when the man with the American accent came up to the table and introduced himself.

'Name's Hank Belding. Understand you guys have a slight problem.'

He was a man of about thirty and there was a lot of him; he was three or four inches over six feet and built like a tank. He had red hair which had not had a pair of scissors within striking distance for many a month, a tangled beard and copper rings dangling from his ears. He was wearing sandals, jeans and a check shirt unbuttoned far enough to reveal an assortment of other hardware in the form of

65

good-luck charms of various kinds hanging from his neck on a metal chain. When he moved he tended to make a slight jingling noise like a draught-horse wearing brasses.

'Problem?' Skene said.

'You aim to get to Laredo but you don't have what it takes in the way of transport. Right?'

'Mr Carrera told you?'

'Sure did.' Belding sat down on a spare chair, making it creak a little. 'He thought maybe I could help.'

'And can you?'

'Put it this way—I have transport. I aim to get to Laredo, too. Maybe we could co-operate.'

'You mean you'd be willing to take us with you?' Holden said.

'It might be arranged. Point is this—I kinda have a problem too.'

'Which is?'

'Empty tank.'

'You're telling us your truck has run out of fuel?'

'Ain't exactly a truck,' Belding said.

'Not a truck! So what is it? A car?'

'Not a car neether. Fact is it used to be a bus.'

Holden stared at him. 'You mean to say you travel around in a bus?'

'Well, it's not exactly a bus now, neether. It's had some alterations made. You'll see.'

66

'I still don't understand what your problem is. You can get your vehicle refuelled right here.'

Belding shook his head. 'There's another slight problem. No bread.'

'Bread?'

'Pesos.'

Holden got the drift of what Belding was saying. 'You're broke?'

'As of this moment in time, yes.'

'Now let's get this straight,' Skene said. 'What you're proposing is that we pay to have the tank filled and you take us to Laredo?'

'Basically, that's it.'

'Basically?'

'There is another small thing—we have to get Brunhilde out of hock first.'

'Who in hell's Brunhilde?'

'My bus.'

'A bus called Brunhilde!' Skene said. 'Now I've heard everything.'

Holden was beginning to wonder whether Belding was not a trifle wrong in the head. 'What do you mean by getting it out of hock?'

'I mean Carlos won't let the old girl go until I pay him for the food.'

'So you've been eating here on credit?'

'You could say that.'

'How did you persuade him to let you do that?'

'I'm supposed to be getting money from the States.'

'And are you?'

'Man,' Belding said, 'there's nobody back there would send me a bent nickel. I could wait here till hell freezes over and nothing would come.'

'You really are in a fix, aren't you? How much do you owe Carrera?'

'Not a lot. A few pesos.'

'What do you call a few?'

'A couple of hundred. Maybe three.'

Holden thought he could see why Carrera was being so helpful to them; it would be to his advantage to have Belding's account settled and get the man off his hands. Maybe he himself was not too hopeful of that money coming from the States.

'No deal,' Skene said. 'We'll get one of the truckers to take us.'

'Three of you? Don't count on it, man. It's against regulations, anyway.'

Holden wondered whether that was the truth. Belding might be saying it just to persuade them to take his offer.

'Why should we bail you out?' Skene said.

'The way I see it, the advantage would be mutual.' Belding appealed to Holden. 'What do you say?'

'I say we ought to take a look at Brunhilde,' Holden said.

The vehicle was standing in a yard at the rear of the filling-station. Belding said it had been there for two days. It occurred to Holden that Belding must have a pretty good appetite if he had eaten his way through three hundred pesos' worth of transport-café food in two days. But he was undeniably a big man and probably burned up a lot of calories.

Brunhilde was a single-decker, old and rather battered, and Belding had not been exaggerating when he had said that it had had some alterations made on it. The alteration that immediately caught the attention was to the exterior paintwork; it looked as though it had been done by an abstract artist under the influence of a large dose of LSD; it really hit you in the eye.

'Like it?' Belding asked.

'It's striking,' Holden said. 'Did you paint it yourself?'

'With some help from like-minded souls.'

'You need your eyes testing,' Skene said. 'Or maybe your brains.'

Belding laughed, taking no offence. 'Let's have a look inside.'

They climbed in. Some of the original seats had been left in the front section but the rest of the interior had had a big conversion job done on it; the seats had been ripped out and some two-tier berths installed on each side of the central aisle, curtained off for privacy—if anyone felt like being private. Further to the rear was a small kitchen with a gas cooker, a sink and some storage lockers. From what he had seen of Belding, Holden would not have expected it to look quite so clean and tidy. Further back still was the toilet.

'Plenty room,' Belding said. 'Suit you guys real fine.'

'There's something I don't quite understand,' Holden said. 'How come you're travelling around in a mobile hotel? Couldn't you manage with something a shade smaller?'

'Thought maybe you'd ask that. Fact is, when we came south five weeks ago this old girl was packed to the gills; you could hardly move for livestock. There was a crowd of us going to a pop festival down in Acapulco.'

'So what happened to the others?'

'They split.'

'Why?'

'Hell, I don't know. What makes people do anything? They just took off and forgot to pay. That's why I'm a mite embarrassed in the financial department.'

'Ha!' Skene said.

Holden could see that he was not favourably impressed with Belding or Brunhilde. Rosita was saying nothing; it was impossible to tell what she was thinking.

'So you've got this monster all to yourself?' Holden said.

'Well, no, not entirely.'

'But you said the others took off.'

'Most of them. Not quite all.'

'So who else is there?'

'Let's go outside and I'll introduce you,'

70

Belding said.

They were standing a few yards away from the bus. There were two of them. Holden understood now about the food bill; they would have been eating too.

'Ruth and Cecile,' Belding said. 'Ruth is my kid sister. Cecile isn't.'

As far as outward appearances were concerned, about the only thing Ruth Belding had in common with her brother was the colour of her hair, and even that was a more attractive shade of red—richer, deeper, like old gold. She was taller than average and slender. She was wearing a long skirt, so that Holden was unable to see her legs, but he would have made a bet that they were just about perfect. All the rest of her was, so why should they be the exception?

The other girl was not quite so tall. She had a snub nose and a wide mouth and large eyes and brown hair cut short in a kind of urchin style. She was wearing shorts and there was a gamine air about her. She was not pretty but she looked the kind of person it might be pleasant to know. It seemed reasonable to guess that she and Hank Belding were lovers. Why else would she have stayed on when the others split?

'You didn't tell us about them,' Skene said. He made it sound like an accusation of double-dealing. He had been pretty sour about Belding's proposal from the start; the revelation that there were two others in the party seemed to make him even more sour.

'I've told you now,' Belding said.

Skene repeated what he had said before: 'No deal.'

'What's eating you?' Belding asked.

'Nothing's eating me but it's still no deal.'

'You won't get a better one.'

'We'll take a chance on that.'

Belding shrugged. 'Please yourself. It's a good offer but you don't have to take it.' He turned his back on them and started to walk away.

'Wait,' Holden said.

Belding stopped and turned to look at him. 'Yeah?'

'Let me have a talk with Harry.'

'Okay, you talk to him. No hurry. We're not going any place.'

Holden put a hand on Skene's arm and drew him to one side, out of earshot of the others.

'I think we should accept his offer.'

'And pay his expenses! No way. We could have gone by train for less.'

'I doubt it. It's not a hell of a lot of money. We can manage it.'

'Sure we can manage it, but I just don't feel inclined to hand out charity to him and his harem.'

'It wouldn't be charity. It would be self-interest.'

'I don't see it.'

'You must be pretty damned blind then,' Holden said, starting to lose patience. 'Can't you see it's our best chance of getting to the United States? To my way of thinking it was a piece of luck running into this party.'

'That may be what you think, but—'

'Hold it now. Just turn your mind for a moment to the subject of the Mexican police.'

'What about the Mexican police?'

'They'll be looking for two men and a girl. Like you me and Rosita. Right?'

'So?'

'So when we get to the border in Brunhilde there won't be two men and a girl; there'll be three men and three girls. It could make all the difference.'

Skene said nothing. Holden could see that he was thinking about it.

'Brunhilde is about the best bit of camouflage we could hope to find,' Holden said.

Skene must have come to the conclusion that there was sense in that, for after a few more moments of consideration he said rather grudgingly: 'Okay; maybe you're right. I still don't like it but maybe it's the best we can do.'

'I'm sure it is,' Holden said.

They went back to the others and told Belding they would accept his offer. Holden thought Ruth and Cecile looked relieved; they were probably sick of hanging around

73

Carrera's place; no doubt they would be glad to get back to the United States.

'I guess you've made the right decision,' Belding said. 'When do you want to start?'

'We're ready when you are,' Holden said.

Half an hour later the financial situation had been straightened out and they were on their way. Brunhilde seemed to be in pretty good running order, considering her age. Belding said he knew plenty about diesels and he would personally guarantee that the engine was up to the mark. Holden hoped he was telling the truth; the last thing they wanted was for the bus to break down somewhere between Mexico City and Monterrey. Belding certainly knew how to handle the big vehicle; which was something to be thankful for.

'I drove a truck one time,' he explained. 'But hell, that's no life. Then one time I was in a harvesting team. We'd start down south in Texas in the early summer and work our way north through the wheat belt until we'd get to Canada in the fall. Man, that job is just one helluva killer, I'm telling you. You gotta keep those machines movin', movin', movin', come hell or high water. Pay's good, but money's not everything.'

'It's ninety per cent,' Skene said. 'Maybe more.'

Riding in the converted bus was no bad way of travelling, Holden reflected. It was a whole lot better than the back of a lorry; the seats

74

were comfortable and if you wanted to get up and move around you could do so. Besides which there was congenial company. He talked to Ruth Belding and found it an enjoyable way of passing the time; she was one really attractive girl.

'You're English, aren't you?' she said.

'That's so.'

'What are you doing in Mexico?'

'Riding in a bus called Brunhilde.'

'You're telling me I should mind my own business?'

'No,' he said; 'it's no secret. Harry and I were seamen on board a freighter. We got left ashore in Puerto Paramo when the ship sailed.'

'I see. Why do you want to get to Laredo?'

'It seemed a good idea to take a look at the United States. Maybe we can pick up another ship in one of the Gulf ports or go north to New York.'

'No other reason?'

'No other reason.'

He was doubtful whether she believed him. She seemed an intelligent girl and perhaps she guessed there was more to it than that. Still, as long as she—and more importantly her brother—did not guess just what that something more entailed, all might be well. He was not sure what course of action Belding would take if he ever got to know about the heroin, but he was quite sure he had no desire to find out.

75

Brunhilde could trundle along at quite a fair pace but it was not to be expected that she would have the speed of a fast car. Belding was not pushing her, anyway; he seemed to be in no hurry to reach the border and Holden could understand that from his point of view there was no need for haste. One thing was certain: they were not going to be in Laredo that day; it was unlikely that they would even reach Monterrey. It was getting well on into the afternoon when the highway began the descent from the central plateau to the basin of the Panuco River, and the air gradually became warmer as the altitude decreased.

'Did you enjoy the festival?' Holden asked.

'So Hank told you about that?'

'Yes. Did you have fun?'

'It could have been better,' Ruth admitted.

Holden gathered that she had not altogether enjoyed it. Maybe there had been some trouble with the others in the party before they took off.

'What will you do when you get back to the States?'

'Who knows? Look around for something.'

'You think Hank will get a job?'

'Maybe you should ask him.'

'Now you're telling me to mind my own business.'

'No,' she said. 'I just don't know what he'll do. We'll need to make some bread somehow. You can't just live on fresh air. I guess you

76

think we're crazy, living like this.'

Holden shook his head. 'I don't think you're crazy. I never had much time for the rat race myself.'

She smiled. 'So it looks like we have something in common.'

'Maybe we have a lot in common,' Holden said. And he hoped there would be time to find out.

They were still a considerable distance from Monterrey when they stopped for the night. Belding said there was no joy in driving on the Pan-American highway after dark; and why bother, anyway? It would still be there tomorrow.

He knew of a camping-site which they had used on the way down. There were a lot of motorised caravans and cars and tents already there but they found room for Brunhilde. A party of young people were having a barbecue and some of them strolled over to take a look at the bus. The paintwork seemed to take their fancy and when they had admired it they invited Hank and the others to join them at the barbecue. The offer of a free meal was too good to refuse and they all went across and joined the party.

It was late when they returned to the bus but they were up early in the morning and were on their way before the barbecue people were awake. They reached Monterrey soon after noon and they stopped there for an hour to get a meal and give the engine a break. By late afternoon they were in Nuevo Laredo. Belding found a quiet place to park the bus and then he got out of the driving-seat and came back to join the others.

'This is the border,' he said. 'On the other side of the Rio Grande is United States territory. You guys wanna split now?'

'Why should we want to do that?' Skene said.

'Just a thought.'

'You're going across, ain't you?'

'Sure. But not today.'

'Why not today?'

'Got a bit of business to do first. There's a man I have to see.'

'You didn't tell us that.'

'Didn't seem important. Just another day. What difference does it make?'

'It could make a lot of difference to us.'

'Could it? Well, it's up to you. If you're in that much of a hurry to go across you don't have to wait. Please yourselves.'

'I think we'll wait,' Holden said.

'Just a minute,' Skene said. 'Since when have you been deciding what we do?' He sounded belligerent and seemed to be looking for an argument.

'I'm not making any decision; I'm just saying I think we should stay with Hank—at least until we're over the border.'

'And I say we should go now.'

78

Belding was watching them with an amused expression. 'If you boys wanna fight about it you'd better do the fighting outside.'

'That just might be a good idea,' Holden said. 'Come on, Harry. I want to talk to you.'

He got down from the bus and walked a few paces away from it. After a brief hesitation Skene followed him.

'Let's have it, then,' Skene said. 'Why do we have to wait another day? We could be in Laredo in half an hour just walking.'

'Perhaps. And perhaps we could be in trouble. We talked about this yesterday, remember? We decided it would be safer to stick with the others until we're safely out of Mexico.'

'Maybe we did. But I didn't know Hank was going to mess around with some personal business on this side of the Rio Grande.'

'What odds does it make? One more day.'

'The sooner we get rid of the heroin, the better.'

'Well, I certainly agree with that. In fact I think we should dump it now.'

Skene stared at him. 'You can't be serious.'

'I am serious. That way we'd be clean.'

'Clean and broke—like Hank. No thanks. Still, if you want to pull out I ain't going to stop you. Rosie and me, we'll take the lot.'

Holden thought about it and was half inclined to cut loose there and then; it would mean a load off his mind. But he could not quite bring himself to do it; he wanted the money.

'No,' he said. 'I'm going through with it.'

Skene grinned. 'I thought you would.'

'But I still say we should go across in the bus.'

'Well, maybe you're right about that.'

'I know I am. And now there's another thing we ought to decide—how we're going to take the stuff through. It'd be asking for trouble to leave it in the luggage.'

'Any suggestions?'

'I've been giving it some thought,' Holden said, 'and this is my idea. Now listen.'

Skene listened.

CHAPTER SIX

A Third of the Take

Holden was coming out of a drugstore where he had been buying a roll of adhesive tape when he thought he saw Marcia Brent, the blonde who had brought the blue Chrysler to them in Puerto Paramo. He could not be absolutely sure it was Miss Brent because he caught only a fleeting glimpse of her as she drove past in an open sports car and she was quickly lost to view in the traffic, but it certainly looked like her.

When he saw her he drew back instantly into a corner of the drugstore doorway. She did not turn her head and he hoped she had not seen him, but he could not be sure about that, either. He wondered what she was doing in Nuevo Laredo—if it was in fact she—and whether Mr Gomez was also somewhere around. The thought made him slightly uneasy and he was still feeling uneasy when he returned to the bus.

The bus was standing on a piece of waste ground on the outskirts of the town where there were some of the kind of shanties that inevitably seemed to spring up on the fringes of all Latin-American towns and cities. In those surroundings Brunhilde attracted no particular interest but seemed to merge into the background.

He told Skene about the blonde.

'You're sure it was the same girl?' Skene asked.

'No, I'm not sure, but it looked like her.'

'Did she see you?'

'I don't think so.'

Skene appeared to be unworried. 'It doesn't matter. Even if it was her it ain't significant. She may have been on her way home to Uncle Sam. Did you get the tape?'

'Yes.' Holden gave it to him. 'When are you going to do the job?'

'Right now. Hank is still away seeing to his business and his two women have gone off

81

somewhere. Couldn't be a more convenient time.'

Belding had told them that he would be ready to take the bus across the border early in the afternoon if that would be all right with them. Skene had said it could not be too early for him, and so it had been arranged.

'I hope this is going to work,' Holden said.

'Well, it was your idea.'

'I know. But things could go wrong. Hank may notice something when he comes back.'

'He won't notice,' Skene said. 'It won't be that obvious.'

'Where's Rosita?'

'She's inside. Let's get the stuff.'

'I just hope it works,' Holden said again.

*　　　*　　　*

If Belding noticed anything he said nothing. It was a little after two o'clock when he got the bus rolling. Not long after that they were crossing the Rio Grande, which the Mexicans perversely insisted on calling the Rio Bravo just to make things confusing. There had been no trouble with the Mexican border officials; if they had in fact been alerted to keep watch for two men and a girl wanted in relation to a fatal accident on the road between Puerto Paramo and Oaxaca they were certainly not looking for them in a jazzy old bus, and Brunhilde went through with scarcely a check. There was a lot

82

of traffic using the bridge in both directions and it had to be kept flowing.

Holden was still worried; it was one thing to get out of Mexico with no bother but quite another matter to get into the United States. But in the event they could hardly have gone through with less friction. The customs check on the vehicle was rapid and somewhat cursory; the luggage was examined and found to contain no contraband, and that was that. Nor was there any difficulty with immigration control; the passports were in order and it was a case of 'Okay, folks. On your way.'

Holden asked Ruth Belding whether it was always as easy as that.

'I don't know,' she said. 'I've only made this one trip south. Hank's been before but I haven't. Were you worried?'

'What makes you ask that?'

'I thought you seemed rather tense, like you might have been expecting trouble perhaps.'

'No,' Holden said, 'I wasn't expecting trouble. I've got nothing to hide.'

'Well,' she said, 'that's nice to know, isn't it?'

He wondered whether she was ribbing him. She was smiling a little, as if amused. He dropped the subject and gazed out of the window at the busy streets of Laredo grilling in the afternoon sun.

Belding shouted back from the driving-seat: 'You guys wanna take a look at the Alamo?'

'No, thanks,' Skene said. 'You can drop us

83

now.'

Belding appeared not to hear him; he just drove on. Skene got up from his seat and went up front to talk to Belding.

'I said you can drop us now.'

'Not yet,' Belding said.

Skene began to argue. He laid a hand on Belding's arm as if to force him to stop.

'I don't think you should let him do that,' Ruth said to Holden. 'He could cause an accident.'

Holden got up and joined Skene. 'Come and sit down, Harry.'

'What's he think he's doing?' Skene said. 'Why won't he let us get off?'

'What's your hurry?' Belding inquired. 'I'll find some place to park and then we can talk things over.'

'There's nothing to talk over.'

'Maybe we'll think of something.'

'What the devil do you mean by that?' Skene was beginning to lose his temper. 'What kind of a game are you playing?'

'Cool it, Harry,' Holden said. 'Why are you getting so upset about nothing? Hank's right; we ought to have a talk before we part company. You can't just step off and leave just like that.'

'You listen to what the man says,' Belding said. He did not turn his head; he needed all his attention for the job of piloting the big vehicle through the mingling traffic of Laredo.

Skene seemed prepared to carry the argument further but thought better of it and allowed Holden to conduct him back to his seat. He was still grumbling, however, and was in no very pleasant mood.

After a while Holden began to wonder just what Belding had in mind; he seemed to be heading out of Laredo and the busy streets had been left behind.

Holden consulted Ruth. 'Do you know where he's going?'

'No, I don't,' she said. 'I've no idea.'

Cecile appeared to be just as puzzled; it was obvious that if Belding had some purpose in his head he had not confided it to them.

'I've had enough of this lark,' Skene said. 'I'm going to get off.'

'You can't,' Holden said. 'Not until he decides to let you.'

There could be no doubt about that. They were quite out of the town now and the bus was moving along at a good speed; anyone who tried leaving it without the driver's co-operation would certainly risk a pair of broken legs and possibly worse.

Skene stood up.

'Now what are you planning to do?' Holden asked.

'I'm going to make that bastard stop, that's what I'm going to do.'

'Sit down. If he doesn't want to stop you can't force him to—unless you're planning to wreck the bus. It isn't going to hurt us to wait a little longer. What are you getting so worked up about?'

'We've got some business to attend to,' Skene said. 'Or had you forgotten?'

'That business can wait. It isn't going to run away. Sit down.'

Skene sat down; but he did so with reluctance, scowling and muttering. Holden could see that he was pretty angry about it all and something was certainly boiling up inside him. He had seen Skene in this sort of mood before and knew how vicious he could be when things were not to his liking. He just hoped Belding would tread softly; if he provoked Skene any further there was no telling what might happen.

About fifteen minutes later Belding slowed down and took the bus off to the left on to a minor road.

'Now where's he going?' Skene said.

'Just wait and you'll be bound to see,' Holden advised him. 'The trouble with you, Harry, is you're too damned impatient. Why don't you remember the old saying about everything coming to him who waits.'

Skene grunted.

The girls were not saying much. Holden had a feeling that they were all a trifle uneasy. Something was happening which they did not understand and perhaps they sensed that the party was going to break up on a sour note.

The road twisted a good deal and there was scarcely any traffic on it. Holden could only suppose that Belding knew where he was going but wherever it was he hoped they would soon get there. And then Belding slowed down again and took a turning to the right which brought them on to a dirt road that looked as though it were very seldom used. In fact there was quite a lot of grass growing on it and there were some tangled plantations of trees on either side which seemed to be encroaching on the road and threatening to block it completely in a few more years if nothing were done to hold them back.

The bus was going slowly and every now and then a low-hanging branch would brush along the roof or the side windows, while small twigs and leaves were broken off in its passing.

'Bloody hell!' Skene said. 'Where the devil is he taking us now?'

He did not have to wait long for an answer; a minute or two later the dirt road came to an end in what appeared to be an abandoned stone or gravel quarry. It was possibly a hundred yards across and on three sides there were cliffs which rose at the highest part to some fifty feet or more. Coarse vegetation of various kinds had sprouted here and there as nature started to repair the damage that man had inflicted on this particular piece of the earth's crust, and in places there had been small landslides where erosion had weakened

87

the cliff.

It was obvious to Holden that Belding must have been there before; he had certainly not driven the bus at random and discovered this place by sheer chance; that would have been too much to believe. But Ruth and Cecile appeared as surprised as anyone, so maybe they were seeing it for the first time.

'Well,' he said, 'it looks as though we're here.'

'And a bloody fine-looking spot it is, too,' Skene said. His face was hard and his eyes had narrowed. Holden knew the signs and he felt certain there was going to be trouble.

Belding drove the bus into the quarry and pulled it to a stop. He opened the door, got out of the bus and walked several paces away from it. Then he turned and waited for the others to join him.

Skene stayed in his seat.

Holden said: 'I think we'd better go and hear what he has to say.' He felt pretty certain now that what Belding had to say would not just be goodbye.

'To hell with it,' Skene said. 'I've got nothing to talk to him about.'

'Do you want to walk all the way back to Laredo?' Holden asked.

'Oh, shit!' Skene said.

He got up from his seat and left the bus. The others followed him.

There was a tumbledown wooden hut on

one side of the quarry and a few pieces of rusting iron lying around. The ground was hard and dry and stony.

'Now, Hank,' Holden said, 'perhaps you'll tell us why you've brought us here.'

Belding grinned. 'Sure, man. Like I said, there's things we have to talk over.'

'What things?'

'Well, for a start maybe you'll give me a straight answer to a straight question. What's your game, fellers?'

Skene gave a sneering laugh. 'That's fine, coming from you. You're the one that's been playing the games, bringing us to this here place. Why'd you do that, hey?'

'It's a good situation for a nice private talk, that's why. No one to overhear what we say.'

'So you knew about this place?' Holden said.

'Oh, sure. I knew it when I was working for my bread. When I was driving a truck like I told you.'

Holden gathered that Belding was familiar with that part of Texas; possibly he was a native of Laredo; he had never told them where he was from and the girls had said nothing on that subject, either.

'And now,' Belding said, 'how about answering my question. What's the game?'

'What makes you think we have a game?'

'Oh, man, you don't fool me. I guessed you were up to something as soon as I laid eyes on you. So now why don't you come clean?'

'I don't know what you're talking about.'

'You don't? Well, maybe the little lady does.' Belding walked across to where Rosita was standing. 'What do you say, honey? Are you going to tell us what goes on?'

'Get away from her,' Skene said.

Belding turned his head. 'Your girl, is she?'

'That's right, and I'm warning you—keep away from her or else—'

Belding seemed unperturbed by Skene's warning and his menacing attitude. 'Put on a bit of weight since she came on board, wouldn't you say?'

Rosita was wearing a kind of short smock over her cotton trousers, hanging loosely at the waist. Belding reached out suddenly and placed his large right hand on her stomach. She stepped back quickly but not quickly enough to avoid his touch.

Belding laughed. 'Wouldn't be having a baby, would you, honey?'

Skene hit him then. Skene was angry and he was a hard hitter. His clenched fist struck Belding in the left side just above the hip. Belding gave a grunt but it did not even stagger him; Skene might have been hitting the trunk of a tree. Belding made a scything movement with his right arm; it was almost nonchalant, like a man swatting an annoying fly, no apparent effort in it. Yet Skene went down and did not immediately get up.

'Don't hit me again,' Belding said. 'Next time I might get angry.' He spoke mildly but the threat was there; he meant what he said.

Skene lay on the ground, staring up at Belding with venom in his eyes. Belding turned his back on him with a kind of contempt.

It was a mistake. Holden was watching Skene and saw him reach for the knife that he carried in a sheath strapped to his right leg just above the ankle. Skene got to his feet with the knife in his hand. One of the girls cried out; it sounded like Cecile. Skene made a rush at Belding but Holden took him from behind, looping one arm round his neck and grabbing his right wrist to prevent him from plunging the knife into Belding's flesh.

Belding had begun to turn when the girl cried out, but he would have been too late if Holden had not intervened; he could have had the knife in him and he might have been a dead man. He must have realised it; he was not laughing now; it was no longer a joke—if it had ever been one. This time he hit Skene on the side of the jaw. Holden felt Skene go limp and the knife dropped from his hand. Skene's whole weight was on his arm; he lowered him to the ground and saw a little trickle of blood at the corner of his mouth. Skene was out cold.

'You didn't have to do that,' Holden said.

Belding agreed. 'I didn't have to but it looked like he was asking for a lesson. That was a real mean trick he pulled.'

Rosita had run forward and was down on her knees beside Skene. Belding reached down and lifted her to her feet.

'Leave him. He'll sleep a bit but he'll be okay. Now what I want you to do is go inside the bus and shed that extra weight you're carrying. You get me, honey?'

She made no move.

Belding said: 'Aw, be sensible. You wouldn't want me to do it for you right here, would you?'

She looked at Holden.

Holden said: 'Better do as he says.' He was not going to fight Belding; it would have been pointless. That way he might end up like Skene, unconscious on the stony ground, and he had no wish to do that.

Rosita began to walk towards the bus. Belding told Ruth and Cecile to go with her to make sure she played no tricks. They were gone for less than ten minutes; when they came back they were carrying the six polythene bags and Rosita was looking thinner in the waist.

'She had these fixed to her with sticky tape,' Cecile said.

Skene had come round and was on his feet but he was not making any aggressive move. He looked groggy and Belding had the knife.

'So,' Belding said, 'you weren't playing any game, huh? You didn't know what I was talking about. So what's in the bags, fellers?

Cooking salt?'

'Okay,' Skene said in a sulky tone of voice. 'Now you know. We were carrying drugs. What are you going to do about it?'

'What sort of drugs?' Belding asked.

'Heroin.'

Belding sucked in his breath sharply. 'Heroin, is it? Don't you know it's a federal crime bringing that stuff into the United States?'

Skene said nothing.

'I think I'll just take a peek at some of this heroin,' Belding said. 'Not that I'm doubting your word, mind; but all the same—'

He took one of the polythene bags, removed the fastening and looked inside. He took a small pinch of the substance between his thumb and forefinger and touched it with the tip of his tongue. Then he refastened the bag.

'Well?' Skene said. 'Are you satisfied?'

'It's not big H,' Belding said.

'Not heroin? What do you know about drugs?'

'Maybe more than you think.'

'And what do you say it is?'

'Coke.'

'You mean cocaine?'

'Sure.'

Holden believed him; it sounded likely. The source of cocaine was South America, especially Peru. Perhaps Gomez had a

93

Peruvian connection; perhaps the shipments came ashore at Puerto Paramo or some place nearby; in small boats maybe. Perhaps Gomez took delivery and channelled the merchandise through Mexico and into the United States. It all fitted in.

Belding looked slightly puzzled. 'I don't get it. How come you guys were smuggling narcotics and didn't even know what sort you were carrying? Makes no kinda sense to me. Tell me.'

'It's a long story,' Holden said.

'Never mind how long it is. Let's have it.'

Holden glanced at Skene.

Skene shrugged. 'He may as well know. No point in keeping it a secret now.' He seemed to have cooled down and become resigned to the situation. He dabbed at the blood on his lip with a handkerchief but when he looked at Belding it was without resentment; possibly indeed with a certain respect.

Holden told the story, keeping it as brief as possible but leaving out nothing of importance.

Belding listened in silence to the end, then laughed.

'What's so funny about it?' Holden asked.

'Maybe you gotta be standing where I am to see it. This Gomez character played you for a pair of real suckers and no mistake.'

'But we had the last laugh,' Skene said. 'We got the cocaine.'

'Nobody's had the last laugh yet,' Belding said. 'You haven't sold it.'

'We will.'

'You think you'll find a buyer?'

'Why not? There's plenty people in the market for this kind of thing.'

'That's for sure, but do you know where to find them?'

'We'll manage,' Skene said.

'Suppose I hand you over to the gendarmes?'

'You wouldn't do that,' Holden said quickly.

'Why not? It's what any upright, law-abiding American citizen ought to do. You might say it's my duty to see you criminals brought to justice.'

'But you're not going to do it.'

'Well, let's put it this way. I'm open to be persuaded not to.'

'What would persuade you?' Skene asked, looking at him very hard.

'A third of the take,' Belding said.

CHAPTER SEVEN

Business Arrangement

Skene let out a yell as if he had been stung by a hornet.

'A one-third share!'

95

'It's reasonable,' Belding said coolly. 'You made use of me without telling me the risk I was taking. And, besides, I could be a lot of help to you guys. I could find you a buyer.'

Ruth broke in quickly then. 'Hank,' she said, 'you promised you'd finished with all that.'

'I know, I know,' Belding said. 'But you have to think of the fix we're in. You have to be realistic. We're down on our uppers and we have to make some scratch.'

'But not this way.'

'It's a chance, honey, a chance. It's too good to let slip.'

'So,' Holden said, 'this upright, law-abiding American citizen has been in the drug racket, has he?'

'I've been in a lot of trades,' Belding said. 'This and that. Sure, I've handled some junk in my time.'

'But you've given all that up,' the girl said, pleading with him. 'Hank, you know you have.'

'Hush now, hush, Ruthie girl,' he said. 'Just this once more won't hurt. Just this once and no more. That's a promise.'

'You promised before.'

'This time it'll be for keeps. Cross my heart.'

She turned away, plainly upset, but apparently accepting the fact that nothing she might say would move him. Holden felt sorry for her but there was nothing he could do to help her; as far as she was concerned he was in the wrong camp—and none too happy about

96

it, either.

'Well now,' Skene said, 'seeing as how you know so much about it, what would you say this little lot is worth?'

Belding weighed one of the bags in his hand and appeared to be making a calculation in his head. Finally he said: 'On the streets I guess it might fetch a million dollars, maybe more.'

Skene gave a long low whistle. 'My, oh my!'

'But don't get any wrong ideas,' Belding said. 'We won't be selling it on the streets. It's got to go through other hands before it gets to the people who use it; so there'll be others wanting their cut. I suggest we ask say two hundred grand.'

Skene's expression changed. A figure of one million had been mentioned but suddenly it was less than a quarter of a million and Belding was claiming a third of that. It was quite a let-down.

'I don't think it's enough.'

'Let's not push our luck,' Belding said. 'You open your mouth too wide and you don't get a sale; you just get six packets of junk on your hands.'

'I think he's right,' Holden said. For his part he would have been glad to be rid of the stuff at almost any price; it bothered him just having it around.

'Well, I don't know,' Skene said. 'I think maybe we should handle it ourselves without him.'

97

'You can't,' Belding said. 'I'm in and you have to accept it. There's no way you're going to squeeze me out unless I want out. But I don't. I want in.'

Holden put a hand on Skene's shoulder. 'Look, Harry, it's a lot of money. Three days ago you would have been happy to take your half of a thousand dollars for delivering a car to Mr Bradley.'

'We didn't know what was in it then. Now we do.'

'It's still a lot of money. It's plenty. Let's not quibble about it.'

'All right,' Skene said reluctantly. 'I can see I'm in a minority of one. I still say it's not enough, but all right, if that's the way it's got to be I'll toe the line.'

'Now you're being sensible,' Belding said.

Skene stabbed the ground with the toe of his shoe. He was far from satisfied but he accepted the situation because he could see no alternative.

'How soon can you contact your man?' Holden asked.

'I'll try tonight,' Belding said. 'It's a while since I was in touch with him but I guess he's still around.'

'Can you trust him?'

Belding shook his head. 'In this game you trust nobody, not even your own brother. It's a jungle. You just have to watch out for yourself and make damn sure the other guy don't put

98

one over on you.'

'What's this man's name?'

'He calls himself Benjamin Sabata but he's known around and about as Benny the Fly. He's a little guy and a fast mover, and what's more he'll suck your blood if you give him half a chance.'

'Which you won't?'

'You bet I won't. He's a small-time operator as these things go. But that's what we're looking for. You go to one of the big syndicates with a job lot like this and they'll laugh in your face, or maybe kick your teeth in. Benny works in partnership with a guy called Finger Malone who supplies the muscle to go with Benny the Fly's brain. He's called Finger because he sometimes pokes his finger in your eye if he takes a dislike to you.'

They sounded like a right pair of villains, Holden thought; but whichever way you turned in this racket you had to be dealing with villains; that was the nature of the business. And maybe Benny the Fly and Finger Malone were no worse than the next lot.

*   *   *

Belding went off by himself in the bus early in the evening. He left the cocaine behind. Skene had insisted on that; he was not going to trust Belding with the merchandise because that way they might never see him again, even though Ruth and Cecile would be staying behind as a kind of guarantee of good faith. Before he left he weighed the polythene bags on the scales in the kitchen of the bus. The weight was fairly close to what he had guessed and he saw no reason to alter his estimate of the value.

He left a pressure lantern so that they would not be in darkness when night fell. They had made an inspection of the hut and had found it to be in rather better condition than might have been expected. There were a lot of cobwebs and dust inside, and not much else except a few empty crates and a rusty iron stove with a flue-pipe going up through the roof. It was not exactly luxury accommodation but they were not planning to spend the night in it.

It was a fine evening, warm and pleasant. Holden decided to go for a stroll to pass the time; there was not much fun in hanging around the quarry just waiting for Belding to come back.

'Where are you going?' Skene asked.

'For a walk. You want to come?'

'A walk!' Skene said. 'Me! Do I look that crazy?'

'It might do you good. A bit of exercise.'

'You can keep your exercise. I'll stay where I am.'

'Please yourself,' Holden said.

He had not walked far down the dirt road

when he heard someone coming up behind him, running. It was beginning to grow dark, and the trees on each side made it even darker, so that it was not until she came up with him that he saw that the person following him was Ruth Belding. He had come to a halt, and she stopped too.

'Do you mind if I come with you?' she asked.

'I'll be glad of your company,' Holden said, with perfect honesty.

He started walking again and she fell into step beside him.

'I'd have invited you to come along, but I didn't think you'd be interested.'

She made no answer to that and they were both silent for a while. Then she said: 'What made you get involved in this drug business, Ray?'

He answered evasively: 'I think you might say it rather crept up on me.'

'But that's no reason. You could have refused to have anything to do with it. Why didn't you?'

He hesitated a moment or two; then said: 'I'll give you a straight answer—greed.'

'Nothing else?'

'No. Just the chance to make some quick easy money and nothing more.'

'You think it's going to be easy?'

'Don't you?'

'I think it could be a long way from easy,'

she said. 'But, easy or not, it's not exactly a nice clean business, is it? Doesn't it give you a bad conscience? Don't you feel the smallest bit guilty about what you're doing?'

'To be perfectly honest with you,' he said, 'I do. But when you're broke and a long way from home and it comes to a choice between an easy conscience and a nice big stack of dollar bills I'm afraid the scales are a bit too heavily loaded on the side of mammon.'

'You disappoint me, Ray. I had a better opinion of you.'

'I'm sorry about that,' he said; and it was the plain truth, because he would have valued her good opinion. 'But I'm afraid that's the way it is.'

'You could still change it. It's not too late.'

'You mean set myself against Harry and your brother? That sounds to me like a recipe for trouble.'

'Are you afraid of them?'

'Afraid? I've never really thought about it. Anyway, Harry's my friend.'

'Do you like him?' she asked. She was not at all averse to putting some pretty blunt questions.

And this was a question he had never put his mind to. He had never asked himself whether or not he liked Skene; they had been thrown together by chance and had interests in common, one of which was to grab some kind of living in an ungenerous world, but that was all. Now, when the question was suddenly put to him, he found himself unable to answer with perfect honesty: 'Yes, I do like Harry Skene.' Indeed there was much about Skene that he certainly did not like, and he had become more and more aware of this in the past few weeks. The fact was that a certain abrasiveness had developed between them. Maybe it was time for the partnership to be dissolved.

'You haven't given me an answer,' Ruth said. 'Never mind; it doesn't matter. I suppose you and he have to stick together. All the same, I do wish you were not mixed up in it.'

'Because it's illegal?'

'Because of that, yes; but also because it's immoral. And, besides, I'm afraid. I don't like violence.'

Holden came to a halt. The girl also stopped and they stood facing each other in the half-light.

'Why should there be any violence?' he asked. 'It's just a straightforward business transaction.'

'In this kind of business,' she said, 'nothing is ever perfectly straightforward; there are too many crooked people involved, too many people grabbing what they can and not caring how they do it, even if it does involve violence.'

Holden thought of the men in the white Citroën. They had been violent, and see where it had got them. She was probably right, too damned right.

'And your friend, Harry,' she said, 'I think he could start some violence, don't you? He's already done something in that line. And why else would he keep a knife strapped to his leg?'

'Self-defence.'

'Do you have one as well?'

'Every seaman carries a knife; it's a tool of his trade. Possibly the most important one.'

'And do you keep yours on your leg?'

'No. And I never carry one when I'm not on board ship.'

'So you do not feel the need for it to protect yourself?'

'Not as much as Harry does.'

She said again: 'I wish you weren't in this, Ray.'

'Why are you so concerned about me?'

'I don't know. I just am.'

He moved closer to her. He put his hands on her shoulders and drew her towards him and kissed her. She seemed to shiver a little, as though she were cold; but he did not believe that was the reason. And she remained passive, neither resisting nor responding. He released her and she moved back a pace.

'Why did you do that?' she asked.

'Because it was something I wanted to do.'

'And did it please you?'

'Not as much as it might have done if there had been more evidence that it was pleasing you.'

'You are not falling in love with me, are you, Ray?'

'I think it would be a very easy thing for me to do,' he said.

'And what good would come of it, do you think?'

'I don't know. You tell me.'

She sighed faintly. 'No good at all, I think. Maybe you had better forget it.'

'And if l don't wish to forget it?'

She turned away from him. 'I think I had better go back to the others now and let you continue your walk.'

'I've lost the taste for it,' Holden said. 'I'll go back with you.'

'If you wish,' she said.

They began to walk back along the dirt road to the quarry.

*   *   *

It was well past midnight when Belding came back with the bus. Holden was relieved to see him and he guessed the others were too. For the latter part of the time they had been congregated in the hut, but it could hardly have been described as a comfortable waiting-room, and conversation had soon flagged.

They all went out to meet Belding when they heard the bus. He switched off the engine and climbed out and they gathered round to hear what news he had to impart.

'You certainly took your time,' Skene said. He sounded peevish and disgruntled, as though it were his belief that Belding had done it on purpose to annoy him.

Belding answered mildly: 'I couldn't manage it any quicker. I had some trouble finding Benny.'

'But you did find him?' Holden said.

'Oh, sure—finally. I ran him to ground in the end.'

They waited for him to go on but he seemed in no hurry to do so; he was a vast shadowy figure in the light from the bus and he just stood there stroking his beard and whistling softly through his teeth, until Skene lost patience.

'Well, come on, for Pete's sake; out with it. Did you do a deal or didn't you?'

'Oh, I did a deal,' Belding said. 'He'll be here tomorrow evening. Ten o'clock.'

Skene seemed disappointed. 'Why didn't he come straightaway—tonight?'

'Look, man, he has to get the cash. You don't think he carries that kinda money around in his pocket? It's not small change, you know.'

'Well, let's just hope he turns up tomorrow.'

'You sound like you think he might not.'

'I won't count on it until I see him.'

'He'll be here. He wants to do business. That's the way he makes his pile.'

'Will he come alone?' Holden asked.

'With that amount of folding money!' Belding said. 'Are you kidding? No way. He'll have Finger Malone with him. And Finger will have a gun. Benny too, or I'm a Dutchman.'

'We'll be taking a risk, then. Both of them with guns and none of us armed.'

'Nobody ever got rich without taking risks.'

'I don't like it,' Skene said.

'Don't worry. It'll be okay. I've had dealings with Benny the Fly before this and I never let him take a bite out of me yet. I don't figure on starting now.'

'Maybe you don't, but—'

'Now hold it, hold it.' Belding seemed to be losing patience with Skene. 'It's all arranged, see? And there's no way you're going to alter it now, no way, man. So you better accept it just the way it is.'

Skene looked very far from being satisfied, but he must have seen that Belding was right; there was no possibility of altering the arrangement now. He might not be happy about it but he had to accept it.

Holden was not at all happy about it, either. From what Belding had said about Benny the Fly and Finger Malone he had gained the impression that they were the kind of people he would much rather not have had any dealings with. People like that were people to stay well clear of; but when you had six bags of cocaine to sell what other kind could you turn to?

'It's late,' Belding said. 'I suggest we all get some shuteye. In the morning things will look better all round.'

Holden doubted it. Belding might be right, and things might turn out fine; tomorrow they might all be a lot richer than they were today; but somehow he just could not bring himself to believe it. When had things ever turned out as sweetly as that?

After turning in he lay on his back for a long time, staring up into the darkness and thinking about the matter, and when he finally fell asleep in the small hours of the morning all the doubts were still in his mind.

CHAPTER EIGHT

Big Hole in the Ground

There was a shower of rain early in the morning and the quarry had the smell that newly dampened ground always has. The rain soon stopped and the sun came out and the earth dried. Steam rose from the roof of the bus and small stones glittered like precious jewels.

They had all slept late; there was no point in getting up early when there was nothing much to do but wait for night to fall.

'Suppose somebody else comes here,'

Holden suggested. 'What then?'

'Who else would come here?' Belding said.

'Campers, maybe.'

'I don't think it's likely.'

'It's possible, though, isn't it?'

'Oh, sure, it's possible; anything's possible. But it's not likely.'

Time passed slowly. They talked.

'Now here's the way we do it,' Belding said. He spelt it out carefully.

Skene raised objections; he disliked Belding's plan and he put forward one of his own. Belding said no, it had to be his way. Holden though Belding was right; he did not want Skene sitting in on the transaction with Sabata and Malone; he was too quick-tempered, too impulsive. As Ruth had said, he could start some violence; and violence was the last thing they wanted.

Skene argued but Holden had the feeling that it was argument for its own sake; he hated to agree with anything Belding suggested. But inevitably in the end he gave way.

'They'd better not be late, that's all.'

'They won't be,' Belding said.

*   *   *

They put out all the lights in the bus half an hour before the time arranged for the meeting. The bus was parked fifty yards away from the hut. Belding and Holden walked across to the hut with the pressure lantern. Holden was carrying a holdall with the bags of cocaine inside it. They went into the hut and Belding hung the lantern on a nail, its hard white light illuminating the interior. Holden put the holdall on one of the crates.

'You don't think we should offer them a bit of light refreshment?' he said. It was just a joke but not very funny. He was not in a laughing mood.

'They won't be expecting anything in that line,' Belding said, not even smiling. 'It's no social occasion. They'll come; they'll take a look at the stuff we have for sale; if they're satisfied they'll hand over the money; then they'll go. That's all there is to it. It should be finished inside ten minutes.'

'You make it sound all so simple.'

'It is simple. Nothing to it.'

Maybe, Holden thought. But he was not convinced. Things were never as simple as that. He looked at his watch; it was twenty minutes to ten. He hoped the men would not be late; it was the devil waiting.

At ten minutes to ten Belding went and stood just outside the open doorway of the hut, his huge body throwing an immense shadow on the ground in front of him. Holden could detect no sign of uneasiness in him but perhaps he was slightly on edge all the same.

More minutes passed. Belding cleared his throat and spat. He shifted his position in the doorway, leaning his back against the jamb, shuffling his feet. Holden picked up the sound of a light aircraft passing overhead. No sound of a car. He looked at his watch again; it was two minutes past the hour.

'They're late.'

'They're here,' Belding said.

Holden looked past Belding and saw the headlights of a car. It was moving slowly, as though the driver were feeling his way carefully. It came off the dirt road and into the disused quarry, the lights picking up the silent bus with its jazzy paintwork, holding it for a moment and then swinging away from it. The car came to a halt some twenty yards from the hut and the lights were dimmed.

'Wait here,' Belding said.

He pushed himself off the doorpost and strolled over to the car. Holden saw two men get out, one of them carrying a black briefcase. They went into a huddle with Belding but he could see no handshaking. Then they all turned and came towards the hut.

When they came in Belding said: 'This is my partner, Ray Holden. He's a Limey, but don't hold it against him; it was an accident of birth. Ray, I want you to meet Mr Sabata and Mr Malone.'

They were much as Holden had expected. Sabata was like a weasel, sharp-nosed, bright-eyed, with slicked-down hair and hardly enough chin for a boxer to have laid a glove

111

on. He was wearing a neat dark suit and fancy shoes. Malone was not as big as Belding but he was big enough; his face was bloated and had the pale look of raw tripe. His hair was cropped short and his jacket was so loose and shapeless it was impossible to tell whether or not he was wearing a shoulder-holster. Holden glanced at his thick, stubby fingers and wondered which of them he used for poking into the eyes of people he did not like.

'A Limey, huh?' Sabata said in a low voice that was scarcely more than a whisper. 'Now ain't that sumpin'.'

He gave a little snigger, as if he found it an amusing state of affairs to be doing business with such a person.

'I bin told,' Malone said, 'as how there's some Limeys is halfway okay.' He made it sound like something he personally found hard to believe. His voice was so thick and hoarse it sounded as though the words had got themselves mixed up with some kind of glutinous substance clinging to the walls of his throat. He glanced at Belding. 'Long time no see, Hank. What you bin doing with yourself?'

'This and that,' Belding said.

'They tell me it's a poor living.'

'Let's have a look at what you're offering,' Sabata said. He seemed to be in a hurry to cut the small-talk and get down to business. Holden thought he also seemed to be slightly nervous. He had set the briefcase down on one of the crates but had not opened it.

Belding opened the holdall and took out the polythene bags. Sabata unfastened one of them, examined the contents closely under the white light from the lantern, tasted a small pinch of the cocaine with the tip of his tongue and gave a nod.

'Okay?' Belding asked.

'I guess so.'

'Where'd you get the stuff?' Malone asked.

'Now,' Belding said, 'you know better than to ask a question like that.'

'It fell off the back of a truck,' Holden said.

Malone grinned. It was not a pretty sight.

Belding looked at Sabata. 'So it's a deal?'

'It's a deal. You'll find the cash in there.' Sabata pointed at the briefcase. 'It's not locked. You better count it.'

Belding released the catches and raised the lid of the case. Holden could see that it was packed with bundles of hundred-dollar bills which looked brand-new. Belding picked up one of the bundles and riffled it with his fingers. His expression changed. He looked at Sabata.

'What's the game, Benny?'

'Game?' Sabata inquired with pretended innocence.

'This is stage money.'

'You don't say. Now there's a thing. And us not even putting on a play.'

Holden noticed with a sense of unease that

113

Malone's right hand had disappeared inside his jacket. Both he and Sabata were standing between the door and the other two.

Belding put the bundle of stage money carefully back with the other bundles in the briefcase.

'So it's a rip-off, Benny.' He sounded cool, a trifle sad, a trifle regretful. 'I didn't expect this from you. I thought you were a straight dealer.'

Sabata gave a shrug. 'Times are hard. Things haven't bin going so good for me lately. I have to do the best I can.'

'So you aim to put yourself back in the money by pulling a fast one on me and my partner. That's not a very friendly act, not friendly at all.'

'I'm sorry,' Sabata said; but his expression belied the words. 'Nothing personal, you understand. A guy has to make a living.'

Holden saw that Malone's right hand had appeared again and that it was gripping a black automatic pistol. And then he saw Sabata haul out a short-barrelled revolver which had been in a holster on his belt. So Belding had been right about them bringing guns. Well, bully for Hank!

'Get the junk,' Sabata said.

Malone picked up the polythene bags and stowed them in the capacious pockets of his jacket. He and Sabata backed towards the door.

114

'Wait,' Belding said. 'You left your briefcase.'

'Keep it,' Sabata said. 'As a souvenir.'

Malone laughed; possibly it all seemed very funny to him. Holden came to the conclusion that Malone's sense of humour was as warped as everything else about him. And yet in a curious way he himself felt a sense of relief; he was glad to see the last of the damned cocaine, and to hell with the money. If those two guns had not been pointing in his direction he might have done some laughing too. But he was not happy about the guns; he had a feeling that Sabata and Malone might take it into their heads to leave a few bullets as souvenirs besides the briefcase, and that these souvenirs might be imbedded in his and Belding's flesh.

'We're leaving now,' Sabata said. 'Don't do anything foolish and you won't get hurt.'

He opened the door and stepped outside. Holden was unable to see precisely what happened then because Malone was blocking the view, but he heard a kind of scuffling noise, a scream and the sound of a pistol shot, which he took to be Sabata's revolver firing once only.

Malone's back had been turned towards the doorway; now he swung round and made a move to go outside. But he never made it; before he could get through the opening Belding was on to him, had an arm round his throat and a grip on his right wrist. Malone

115

struggled violently but the big man was too strong for him.

'Cool it,' Belding said. 'Cool it.'

And then Holden caught a glimpse of Skene with the knife in his hand, the blade dripping blood. He saw what Skene was about to do and he shouted at him in an attempt to avert it.

'No, Harry, no!'

But Skene was not listening. He made a vicious thrust with the knife and Malone stopped struggling. Belding let go of him and Skene moved quickly out of the way. Malone fell forward out of the hut and lay on his face in the dirt.

'Well,' Belding said, 'now you've really done it, haven't you? I guess you've killed them both, Harry. You sure are a one with that slicer.'

'The bastards,' Skene said. 'They thought they'd cheat us, did they?'

'So you heard?'

'I heard,' Skene said. 'Oh, I heard all right.' He stepped over Malone's body and came into the hut. 'You picked a fine pair of villains to make a deal with, and that's a fact. I could've been killed, do you know that? That bloody little rat nearly shot me.'

'But he didn't.'

'No thanks to you.' Skene had had a close call and he was angry. There was a lot of blood on his right hand but none of it was his. He was no longer holding the knife, so it was

116

probably still imbedded in Finger Malone's flesh.

'God!' Holden said. 'Now we are in trouble. Why in hell did you have to use the knife?'

It had not been part of the plan. Skene was to have waited outside the hut, keeping out of sight, and in the event of things going wrong he was to have slugged the men with a baseball bat as they came out. The bat was one Belding kept in the bus as a handy weapon in case of emergencies. But of course Skene had altered the scenario, had used a more lethal weapon; and now they had two dead men on their hands. God, what a mess!

'They had guns, didn't they?' Skene said. 'They got what they asked for. Bastards.'

There were sounds outside, voices. The girls must have heard the shot and had come out of the bus to see what was happening. It had certainly been a shock to find two dead bodies lying in front of the hut. The gruesome sight had brought them to an abrupt halt.

Belding went to the doorway and spoke to them. 'Go back to the bus. There's been some trouble but none of us is hurt. There's nothing you can do here, so go back to the bus. Make some coffee, and make it strong.'

He had authority; they turned and walked away, not saying a word, probably scared dumb.

'What do we do now?' Holden said. He thought of the police; something like this ought to be reported to them. But he saw that there was no way he was going to sell that idea to Skene and Belding; he was not even sure he could sell it to himself. How did you start explaining away two dead men and six bags of cocaine to unbelieving cops?

'What we do now,' Belding said, 'is start digging a big hole in the ground.'

CHAPTER NINE

QUESTION OF BUSINESS

Holden slept badly. He had unpleasant dreams and when he woke in the morning he felt unrefreshed. He doubted whether any of the others had had a very good night's sleep, either. Breakfast could hardly have been described as a lighthearted meal and only Skene and Belding appeared to have much appetite. The sight of the green Ford which Sabata and Malone had arrived in, still standing where it had been parked, was an unwelcome reminder of what had happened the previous evening. Not that anyone needed reminding.

'Now,' Belding said, when they had finished the meal, 'I guess we'd better have a talk about what the next move is to be. It looks like we gotta look for another buyer for our merchandise.'

Holden stared at him unbelievingly. 'Are you saying we should go on with this? After what's happened.'

Belding appeared surprised at such a question. 'What else? What are you suggesting we do?'

'Throw the damned cocaine away and forget the whole thing.'

'That would be pretty damned silly, wouldn't it? We've come this far; we're in up to the neck whichever way you look at it. No point in pulling back now. We have a saleable commodity and we better sell it.'

'Too true, we'd better,' Skene said.

But Ruth said softly: 'I think we should do as Ray suggests.'

Belding turned to her. 'Now, Ruth honey, that's just plain foolishness, and you must know it is.'

'You wouldn't be thinking by any chance of handing me over to the coppers, would you, Miss Belding?' Skene inquired with a sneer. 'Because I can tell you it's just not on. Your brother is in this as deep as I am; he held Malone while I put the knife in, so there's no way he can get out of it. If I go down, he goes down with me. And Ray too, if it comes to that.'

She looked at him with an expression of disdain but made no answer.

'Okay, okay,' Belding said. 'We get your

point. But nobody's going down and nobody's going to the cops. Forget it.'

Cecile and Rosita were saying nothing but they looked pretty sick; and frightened too. Holden wondered whether the Mexican girl was regretting that she had persuaded Skene to bring her along. It had all seemed like a lot of good fun at the time but there was not much fun left in it now; the fun had started to go out of things when the white Citroën got on their tail on the road to Oaxaca, and matters had gone from bad to worse since then.

'Let's make a run-down of our assets,' Belding said. 'We now have the use of a car; we have two guns and some ammo; and we have one hundred and nine dollars in cash— besides what you guys have left.'

The extra dollars had come from the wallets of Benny the Fly and Finger Malone. Taking them had been robbing the dead; but, as Belding had said, what sense would there have been in burying the cash with them? That sort of caper was for Egyptian Pharaohs, not for dime-a-dozen American hoods.

'You'd have thought they'd've had more than that on them,' he said. 'It's not much. So maybe Benny was telling the truth when he said times were bad. Maybe there was no way he could raise that two hundred grand in real bills.'

'It'll be a sight worse for him where he's going,' Skene said.

They had buried the two men at the foot of the cliff on one side of the quarry. A big chunk of earth and stone had been ready to fall at that point, and they had given it some help and it had come down with a rush, completely obliterating the new grave. It looked like a natural fall and provided the perfect camouflage.

'People are bound to be looking for them,' Holden said. To him it seemed crazy to talk of going ahead with the operation and even to suggest using Sabata's car. 'People will wonder why they're not around any more. There'll be police inquiries.'

'No,' Belding said, 'that's not so. Why would anyone go looking for guys like them? They were loners; they didn't even have wives and families. Sure, somebody may notice they're not around and about, but that won't cause any talk; there could be pretty good reasons why they'd want to disappear. You can bet your boots nobody will go to the cops, because the kind of citizens who knew them don't go to the cops about anything.'

He could be right, Holden thought; but he was not happy about it. He had been happier when he was down to his last peso in Puerto Paramo before ever Señor Gomez had appeared on the scene and made his offer. That damned bastard, Gomez.

'The question now,' Belding said, 'is who do we offer the coke to next?'

Skene made a suggestion. 'I vote we contact Mr Bradley. We know he wants it.'

Belding tugged at his beard and looked thoughtful. 'Now that really could be dangerous.'

'It'll be dangerous whichever way we do it. And Bradley might be only too glad to cut his losses by taking the stuff at a reasonable price.'

'It is just possible at that,' Belding admitted. 'On the other hand he's likely to be sore, real sore.'

'So he's sore. Let him be. I still say he'll do a deal.' Skene appealed to Holden. 'What do you say?'

'I say it's crazy.'

'You're wrong. It's the way we get paid off.'

'It could be the pay-off all right.'

'Where's this Mr Bradley hang out?' Belding asked.

'A place called Briggsville,' Skene said. 'Ever hear of it?'

'Sure. I know Briggsville. It's north of here, a little one-horse town. Not the sort of place you'd expect a big operator to hang out.'

'Well, that's where we were told to deliver the Chrysler.'

'There's one thing,' Belding said, still thinking about it; 'that way we don't need to go into Laredo, and it might be better to stay clear of there for the present; specially if we're using Benny's car.'

'So Briggsville it is?' Skene said.

'I guess so,' Belding agreed. 'But there's just one other point. With Bradley I think we should cut the asking price to one hundred and twenty grand.'

'Why?'

'It mightn't pay to push him too hard. The way he'll look at it, it's his coke, and he'll find it hard enough to swallow having to buy it back anyway. A hundred and twenty makes forty for each of us. That's good money. What do you say?'

Skene was reluctant but after some more argument he accepted that Belding was possibly right about not pushing Bradley too hard.

Belding turned to Holden. 'That suit you, Ray?'

'None of it suits me,' Holden said. 'But I suppose that's the way it has to be.'

He did not look at Ruth; he did not wish to see the expression on her face, did not wish to meet her gaze. He knew what he would have read in her eyes and he did not wish to read it.

*   *   *

The Red Ace garage was on the far side of Briggsville, which was a town that in Holden's opinion merited Belding's unflattering description. As far as he could see there was very little to recommend it, but no doubt the inhabitants would not have agreed. Maybe

123

they thought it was a great place in which to live; and they had erected a sign which read: 'Welcome to Briggsville. A Mighty Fine Town. Population 2506'.

The garage was not quite in the mighty fine town; it was on a rather second-class road about half a mile out. It seemed to be built mainly of timber and corrugated iron and dirty glass, and it had certainly been there a good many years; time enough for the iron to rust and the timber to rot and some of the glass to get itself broken. It looked the kind of place that might have been reasonably thriving until somebody decided to build a new road and leave it in a sort of traffic backwater; but now it gave the impression of having quietly given up the struggle. It was old, ugly and depressing and to Holden it seemed that the best thing that could have been done to it would have been to sprinkle it with petrol and strike a match.

Belding had led the way to Briggsville in Brunhilde. The other two men had followed in Sabata's car with Skene driving. The girls were with Belding.

When they came to the Red Ace garage Belding drove on, and very soon the bus was out of sight. Skene steered the green Ford on to the weedy forecourt and brought it to a halt. He switched off the engine and sounded the horn.

'There's something screwy about this,'

Holden said. 'I don't like the look of it.'

There were some old cars parked on one side of the garage; weeds were growing round them and they looked as though they had been dumped there. One of them had a crushed radiator and bonnet, possibly the result of a head-on collision or an argument with a brick wall. Beyond the cars were some empty oil-drums and a stack of worn-out tyres.

'Where in hell is everybody?' Skene said. He gave another long blast on the horn.

This time he was successful in attracting attention. A man came out of the garage, yawning, as though he had been roused from sleep. He was a tall, thin, middle-aged man in greasy denims and a peaked cap. He had a stringy neck and a prominent Adam's apple and there was a lot of grizzled stubble on his cheeks and chin. He looked at the Ford and then started walking towards it. Skene and Holden got out and waited for him.

'You want some gas?' the man asked.

'No,' Skene said.

'What you want, then?'

'Mr Bradley.'

The man's head jerked a little and the strings in his neck tightened. He treated the others to a closer and more searching scrutiny than he had given them before. He seemed suspicious, a trifle wary.

'Who are you?'

'My name's Skene; he's Holden,' Skene

125

said.

'Where are you from?'

'Mexico.'

'Who sent you?'

'Mr Gomez.'

The man glanced at the car, gave Skene and Holden another hard look; then said: 'You shoulda bin here four, five days ago.'

'We had some trouble. It delayed us a little. We're here now.'

'What orders did Mr Gomez give you?'

'He said we were to deliver the car to Mr Bradley. Then we'd be paid.'

'That the car?'

'That's it.'

'Don't look like no blue Chrysler to me.'

'So?'

The man sucked his teeth and spat. 'Way I heard it, it was to be a blue Chrysler. This here automobile looks like a green Ford to me.'

'That's what it looks like to me, too.'

'So how come?'

'Never mind how come. Are you Mr Bradley?'

'No, I ain't. My name's Crane.'

'Is Mr Bradley here?'

'No.'

'Well, can you tell us where we can get in touch with him?'

Crane scratched his stubbly chin and looked doubtful. He glanced again at the Ford; the fact that it was not a Chrysler obviously

126

bothered him. At last he said:

'I'll have to make a telephone call. You wait here.'

'Will you be speaking to Mr Bradley?'

'Mebbe.'

'Tell him we've got what he's looking for.'

'And what would that be?'

'He'll know.'

Crane went away muttering under his breath and disappeared inside the garage building.

'This isn't going to work out, you know,' Holden said. He felt uneasy; his inclination was to get back into the Ford and drive away before Crane returned.

But Skene appeared not to share his misgivings. 'It'll be all right. Don't worry.'

'That man is suspicious.'

'It doesn't matter. He's not important. You can see he's just a link. When we get to see Mr Bradley, that's when we start to talk business.'

Holden thought it could be bad business but he said nothing more; things would have to take their course now and, if they turned out badly, so be it.

A few minutes later Crane came back.

'Well?' Skene said. 'Did you talk to him?'

'I talked to him.'

'What did he say?'

'He said he'd see you.'

'That's more like it. Is he coming here?'

'No, he never comes here. You'll have to go

127

to his place.'

'Where's that?'

'I'll tell you how to get there,' Crane said.

*　　　*　　　*

The bus was parked at the side of the road half a mile or so beyond the garage. They pulled the car in behind it and went to tell Belding what had happened.

'It's about what I expected,' he said. 'I doubt whether that guy, Crane, knows much of what goes on. He's small fry. You turning up late with the wrong car threw him, I guess; but it's not important; the game's out of his hands now. From here on in we deal with the bigger fish. You reckon you can find the place?'

'You think we're dumb?' Skene said. ' 'Course we can find it.'

'Okay; it was just a question.'

'Where will you wait for us?' Holden asked. 'Here?'

'No. We'll go back to the quarry. No sense in hanging around these parts. You know what you have to do.'

'Oh, we know,' Skene said.

'On your way, then. And the best of luck.'

'We may need all that's going,' Holden said.

*　　　*　　　*

It took them half an hour to get there. Over

the gateway there was a big painted sign which read: 'Hornsby Stud Ranch', but there was no name of Bradley on it. There were a lot of white-painted post-and-rail fences and acres of good green pasture with shade trees dotted around here and there, and there was a winding private road leading to the house and the stables and barns and other buildings. It all looked very well-kept and prosperous, and Holden remarked that there must be plenty of profit in the horse-breeding business.

Skene gave a sardonic laugh at that.

They drove up to the house, which was a big rambling timber building in the southern style. There was a wide terrace all along the front, with a row of white pillars supporting the roof and coloured tiles underfoot. Scattered around were lounging-chairs and a table or two, and there was some trellis-work with creepers growing up it and bursting into flower all over the place.

There was a young woman sitting on one of the chairs. She stood up when Skene and Holden got out of the car and walked up to the terrace. She was wearing a plain white summer dress and tinted glasses, and she had long blonde hair and a nice line in suntans.

'Well,' she said, 'so here you are; you finally made it. You had us worried, you know. We were beginning to think we'd lost you.'

'We're not so easy to lose,' Skene said. 'We're like bad pennies; we have a way of

129

turning up. It's nice to see you again, Miss Brent. I hope you had an easier journey than we did.'

'So you had trouble?' she said. 'We'll have to talk about that.' She glanced at the green Ford. 'That doesn't look like the car you had from me.'

'It ain't,' Skene said. 'We'll have to talk about that as well. But maybe not to you.'

'No?'

'No. The character we'd like to talk to is Mr Bradley. Not that it wouldn't be very nice talking to you, of course, but he's the one we really came to see. It's a question of business.'

'Ah!' she said. 'Business. Yes, that's about what it would be. Well, we'd better go inside.'

She turned and led the way into the house, into a spacious hall from which a wide banistered staircase ascended to a gallery. There was an impression of opulence, of easy living; there were expensive draperies, much polished wood, a feeling of air-conditioned luxury.

'This way,' Miss Brent said.

She left them in a room with a view of a swimming-pool which no one was using. It looked like a Hollywood film set waiting for the actors and actresses to come and animate it. There were diving-boards and chairs and tables and sun-shades, and not one suntanned body in sight. The water was pale green and the sunlight glinted on its surface.

130

'It'd be nice to have a swim,' Holden said.

Skene agreed. 'But we don't have the time, pal. We have a job to do.'

There was a big open fireplace, all wrought-iron and blocks of white stone. Above the fireplace was an oil-painting; a man mounted on a horse. They sat in leather-upholstered armchairs and waited for Mr Bradley to put in an appearance.

When the door opened there were three of them who came in. The first was Marcia Brent and she was followed by a sturdy broad-shouldered man of about sixty with thick silver-grey hair which looked as though it had just come from the barber's hands. The man's face was square, bony, the nose prominent, the skin gathered into a web of tiny wrinkles, the eyes ice-blue and deep-set. Holden saw immediately the resemblance to the man in the painting, though that one, to judge by his dress, had been of an earlier generation.

The third person to enter the room was no stranger to Skene and Holden. It was Mr Gomez, whom they had last seen in a cantina in Puerto Paramo in southern Mexico.

CHAPTER TEN

NOT THE TYPE

The grey-haired man introduced himself. 'I am Charles Hornsby. You have, of course, already met my niece, Miss Brent, and Señor Gomez.'

'Yes, we've met them,' Skene said; and he took a good hard look at Gomez, who seemed to Holden to be not altogether at his ease; a trifle nervous perhaps, as though not particularly happy about meeting the two Englishmen again in these surroundings.

'Then there is no need for any further introduction,' Hornsby said. He sat down, and Marcia Brent and Mr Gomez did the same. 'Now we will have our little talk if you gentlemen are quite ready.' He was very polite, very soft-spoken; he might have been welcoming a couple of old friends to a cosy little chat. But there was really nothing cosy about it and Holden was pretty sure they all knew it.

'Now just wait a minute,' Skene said. 'Begging your pardon, Mr Hornsby, but it ain't you we came to talk to; we're looking for Mr Bradley and I don't see him around.'

Hornsby smiled very faintly. 'There is a good reason for that. Mr Bradley, you see, does not in fact exist; he is simply a name, a

132

figment, one might say, of the imagination. Do you understand?'

Skene understood. 'Oh, I get it. We talk to you, and that's the same as talking to Mr Bradley.'

'Precisely. And perhaps it would be best if you started by telling us what happened to the Chrysler.'

Skene told him, turning to Holden now and then for corroboration. Hornsby listened in silence and it was apparent that Gomez was listening intently, too—and perhaps not caring a great deal for what he heard.

When Skene had finished his story Hornsby said: 'It seems to me you two boys are lucky to be alive.'

'You can say that again,' Skene said.

Hornsby took a cigar from his pocket and lit it. Then he said: 'Now I'll tell you a very curious thing: this is the third time something of the sort has happened; but on the two previous occasions nobody turned up here to tell the tale. Now what do you make of that, Mr Skene?'

'Why, Mr Hornsby, it looks like somebody down in Mexico is doing the dirty on you by hijacking your car shipments. That's about the way I see it.'

'Yes, it really does look like that, doesn't it? But the question is, how would they know about those shipments, do you think?'

'Now that's something I can't rightly tell

133

you,' Skene said. 'But if I was you I'd take a good close look at the Mexican end of my organisation, because it's pretty damned certain there's been a leakage of information somewhere down that way.'

Gomez was beginning to look very uncomfortable indeed, and now he broke into the conversation. He said: 'There is no reason to suppose that. There is a large amount of car-stealing goes on down there, the same as everywhere else these days. We have simply been unfortunate, that is all. What I say is—'

Hornsby was looking at him and he broke off as if he had suddenly forgotten what it was he was going to say. He was sweating a little in spite of the air-conditioning.

'You are right,' Hornsby said. 'We have been unfortunate—most unfortunate. And that kind of misfortune cannot be allowed to continue.' He shifted his gaze back to Skene. 'But you have not told us the complete story, have you? You have not told us what you did with the Chrysler after you left the scene of the crash.'

'We took it apart,' Skene said.

'Ah! And why did you do that?'

'Because nobody steals a car the way those characters in the Citroën were doing it, not even in Mexico. So they had to be after something in the car. And I don't mean the passengers.'

'And when you took the car apart, did you find anything interesting?'

134

'You bet your sweet life we did. Six polythene bags full of cocaine.'

Hornsby gave no indication of being at all surprised by this revelation. He had known it, of course, ever since he had received the telephone call from Crane with the message that Skene had given. There was only one thing that message could mean, though Crane might not know it.

There was a brief silence, nobody saying a word. It was Hornsby who broke it. He said: 'And now you have brought this cocaine to me?'

'Well, it's you it was meant for, ain't it?' Skene said. 'So who else should we bring it to?'

'How very honest you are!' Hornsby said; and there was not even a hint of sarcasm in his voice.

'Well, there's something owing to us, ain't there?' Skene said, with a grin.

'Ah, I take it you are alluding to the six hundred dollars you were to be paid on delivery.'

Skene grinned again, not very pleasantly. 'You have to be joking, Mr Hornsby. After all we've been through you can't really expect us to settle for a miserable six hundred bucks. You ain't that dumb.'

Hornsby's expression did not change; he had absolute control over himself and he spoke as mildly as ever. 'So you think your services are worth rather more than that. Have

135

you any figure in mind?'

'Yes, we do have a figure in mind. One hundred and twenty thousand.'

Marcia Brent laughed; she seemed really amused. Gomez did not laugh and he did not look amused; he was finding nothing at all funny in the proceedings. Holden guessed that he would rather have been somewhere else, maybe a thousand miles away.

Hornsby said: 'Dollars, of course?'

'American dollars,' Skene said.

'Mr Skene,' Hornsby said, 'it is you who are dumb if you think for one moment that I will pay you that kind of money.'

Skene suddenly looked far less pleased with himself. He must have thought he had Hornsby going, almost eating out of his hand, and now he had received this smack in the face. Holden had never believed it; he had looked into Hornsby's eyes and seen how hard and cold they were, and he had not been deceived by the mildness of his words and manner. There was nothing soft about Hornsby and he was so confident of himself that he felt no need to raise his voice or show his anger.

Skene lacked any similar control. He said with a little spurt of venom: 'You'll bloody have to if you want the stuff.'

'Is that so?' Hornsby said. 'Now isn't there a certain point that appears to have escaped your notice? Wasn't it rather simple-minded of

136

you to come here and place yourselves in my hands?'

Skene laughed jeeringly. 'You think we brought the coke with us? Not likely. And I'll tell you something else: there ain't just the two of us in this now; we've got partners. So don't think you can use the strong-arm lark on us, because it won't work. Either you pay us what we're asking or we go to another customer, see?'

'I am rather surprised,' Hornsby said, 'that you came to me at all.'

'Well, you know how it is. We reckoned as how you should have the first offer.'

'How very considerate of you!' Hornsby said. And he was certainly not believing a word of it.

'So now is it a deal or isn't it?'

'I shall have to think about it. It's not something to be decided all in a moment.'

Skene was not pleased and his face showed it. He seemed about to make an answer when he was stopped by the sound of a knock on the door and then the door opened and two men came in.

Holden took one look at them and knew they were no ranch-hands. He doubted whether they could have told one end of a horse from the other unless it bit them. They were just toughies; Hornsby's bodyguards perhaps; the boys who did any dirty work that might be needed. They looked capable enough in that line.

'Well,' Hornsby said.

The one who answered was dark, slightly balding, thick round the waist, fortyish. He had a small scar above his left eye and he blinked when he talked.

'Nothing there, Mr Hornsby. Nothing at all.'

'You're sure?'

'You can trust us, Mr Hornsby,' the other man said. He was younger, taller, not so thick in the waist. His hair was so pale it looked as though it had been bleached, and it came down over his ears like a curtain. 'We went through it good. There's no way it could be there.'

'Well now,' Skene said, 'what's all this? So you thought we had it in the car and you told these goons to make a search. You must think we're green.'

'No,' Hornsby said, 'I didn't think it would be there, but it would have been foolish to ignore the possibility. I don't take chances; I make sure.'

'Good for you. So now what's your answer to our proposition?'

'I told you before; I shall have to think about it.'

'You'd better not take too long about it. We haven't got all the time in the world.'

'Very well; I'll give you my decision tomorrow. Call me on the telephone at eleven o'clock in the morning and you'll have my answer.'

'Okay,' Skene said. He got up from his chair. 'We'll be going, then—if there's nothing else you want to say.'

'There is one other thing. I'm afraid one of you will have to stay here.'

It set Skene back on his heels. 'Now what in hell's this all about? What you mean, one of us will have to stay?'

'Purely as a guarantee of good faith.'

'You mean you're aiming to keep one of us here as a hostage?'

Hornsby made a slight movement with his hand as though dismissing such a coarse suggestion. 'Not a hostage; let us say a guest. Whichever of you elects to stay will find it very comfortable here, I do assure you.'

'Well, let me tell you something,' Skene said, thrusting his jaw out belligerently; 'neither the one nor yet the other of us is staying. We're both leaving now and nobody'd better try and stop us.'

He took a couple of steps towards the door and the men he had called goons moved to block his way. He dipped a hand into his pocket and hauled out the snub-nosed revolver that had been Benny Sabata's; but he had hardly got it into view when the scarred man hit his wrist with the barrel of a big black automatic and the other man twisted his left arm up behind his back. They did it all quickly and without trouble and the scarred man took the revolver from him and dropped it into his own pocket. Skene started swearing, but he was helpless against the two of them, and Holden was not fool enough to go to his aid, because he had no weapon and the least he was likely to get for his pains was a smack on the head with that big pistol that the scarred man was holding.

'Now really, Mr Skene,' Hornsby said, 'don't you think that was very foolish of you? This is just the kind of thing Morton and Katz are employed to do. They're experts. You should never have pulled the gun, you know. You shouldn't even have brought it here.'

'Go to hell,' Skene said.

'Which is no doubt where you'd like to send me at this moment. But not yet, my friend, not yet.' Hornsby looked at Holden. 'Have you also got a gun?'

'No,' Holden said. 'I never use them.'

Hornsby seemed to accept his word for it. 'So now which of you is going to stay? It has to be one of you.'

'I'll stay,' Holden said. He could not have explained just why he made the offer and he half regretted it as soon as the words had left his mouth, but he could not back out then.

'All right,' Skene said, agreeing quickly, as if to make sure that Holden had no time to change his mind. 'Now give me back my gun and I'll be on my way.'

'No gun,' Hornsby said. 'I guess you're safer

without one. Seems to me you have a mighty quick temper.'

Skene looked like showing that quick temper again but he controlled himself. At a word from Hornsby the fair-haired man released his arm and opened the door. Skene went out with the fair-haired man closely following, no doubt to conduct him safely to the car.

'Your friend is a very impulsive man,' Hornsby said. 'He's likely to get himself into bad trouble one of these days. Katz could easily have broken his arm, you know.'

'I don't doubt it,' Holden said. And he was thinking that Skene could get other people besides himself into trouble, and already had.

The rest of the day passed slowly. He was allowed to wander around more or less as he chose, but either Katz or Morton was never very far away and it was obvious that he was not going to be given any chance to escape. In the afternoon Marcia Brent came and talked to him.

'Do you like it here?' she asked; and he thought he detected a faint note of mockery.

'I might like it better,' he said, 'if I were a willing guest and not a prisoner.'

'But I thought you were willing. Didn't I hear you offer to stay?'

'Only because it had to be one of us and I could see that Harry was not going to be happy if he was the one who stayed behind.'

141

'So you sacrificed yourself for your friend? That was noble of you.'

'You're laughing at me,' he said. 'It must seem very amusing to you.'

'A little,' she admitted. 'Tell me, are you interested in horses?'

'Not wildly. But if you're offering to show me some I'll accept the offer. It'll help pass the time.'

She smiled. 'Not the most gracious way of accepting, but no doubt you're not in a gracious mood. Come along, then.'

They did a tour of the stables, which looked a lot more habitable than many of the dwellings he had seen whole families living in down in Mexico; but no doubt these horses were more valuable, head for head, than those people, and therefore warranted better accommodation. He was no judge of horseflesh but to his untutored eye the Hornsby stud looked good. There were a few men working around the yards and stables; they looked a different breed from Morton and Katz and he wondered whether they knew what kind of business the boss had his fingers in besides the horse-breeding one. Even if they guessed, maybe they kept it to themselves, content to do the jobs they were paid to do and not ask any questions about where the money came from. But more likely they knew and suspected nothing.

'There've been Hornsbys here for

generations,' Marcia said. 'This place has been handed down from father to son since I don't know when.'

'Were they all crooks?' Holden asked.

She frowned at that. 'You're a crook yourself, Ray Holden; so don't be snooty.'

He could not deny it. By bowing to Skene's persuasion it was what he had made himself and he was in no position to criticise anyone else for dishonesty.

Later she asked him how he came to be a seaman. 'Somehow you don't strike me as quite the type.'

'Is there a type?'

'Perhaps not. But you're not much like Skene, are you? For one thing I'd say you were better educated.'

'I suppose that's true. The fact is I'm a bit of a drop-out. I might have been a lawyer like my father but somehow it didn't appeal to me. I've knocked around a bit, doing this and that, nothing very lucrative.'

'How does it feel to be a drop-out?'

'At the present time, none too good.'

'Maybe it'll get better. You could get to be rich.'

She was mocking him again and he knew it. She did not believe he would get rich; she did not believe this thing would work out in his favour. Maybe she knew her uncle too well. His own impression of Hornsby was of a man who did not care to lose and would do his damnedest to ensure that he did not.

'I'll never be rich,' he said. 'I'm not that type, either.'

*   *   *

Katz came up with him when he went to bed. He thought perhaps Katz was going to sleep in the same room to keep an eye on him and was pleased to find that this was not so. But he heard the key turning in the lock on the other side of the door and knew that they were still taking no chances.

It was a nice room, no doubt about that. It had its own bathroom and there was an electric razor for guests like him who had omitted to bring their own toilet gear. There was a suit of pyjamas laid out on the bed and there were some glossy magazines on the bedside table in case he felt the need for some light reading. It was all very cosy and would have been pleasant enough if he had been able to forget the painful fact that he was not really a guest but a captive.

He went to the window and found that there was a balcony outside. He stood on the balcony and looked down, and the ground did not seem so very far below him. There were lights showing here and there, and beyond the lights the darkness closed in. It would, he thought, be not too difficult to hang from the balcony by his hands and drop to the ground.

144

But perhaps somebody had been told off to keep watch out there; they would hardly make it quite so easy for him to escape. Still, it would be worth trying later in the night, and if he succeeded in getting away he would make his way back to the quarry and tell the others that he was pulling out. They could go on with the scheme if they wanted to but he would take no more part in it. He would break away from them and, if Ruth Belding liked to come with him, she could. But one way or the other he would have no more of it.

He did not feel much like sleeping; he was too wound up. But he undressed and got into bed, and he looked at some of the magazines and after a time the print started to blur, so he switched the light off and lay back on the pillow. He would wait a couple of hours or so and then he would get up and put his clothes on again and make the escape attempt. It would be about two o'clock in the morning by then and if anyone was keeping watch the man would be pretty sleepy, so with luck he might make it.

He had not intended to close his eyes but he did so without being aware of it. By that time he had ceased to be much aware of anything, and it was a very comfortable bed, very comfortable indeed . . .

CHAPTER ELEVEN

FULL PARTNER

He did not hear the key turn in the lock and he did not even hear the door opening. The first thing he knew was that somebody was shaking him and saying:

'Wake up, Ray. It's time to get up.'

He opened his eyes and saw Marcia Brent leaning over the bed. She was wearing a white towelling bathrobe and her hair was swept back from her forehead and tied in a pony-tail at the back. When she saw that he was awake she stopped shaking him and stood back, smiling.

'What time is it?' he asked. And suddenly he remembered the escape attempt he was to have made and had never got around to making. He must have fallen asleep and slept right through. Which was a damned idiotic thing to have done, for he had certainly lost all chance of getting away now.

'It's eight o'clock,' she said. 'I thought you might like to join me for a swim.'

The bathrobe was not fastened and he could see that beneath it she was wearing a scarlet bikini of fairly minute proportions. All that was visible of her skin had a beautiful golden tan.

146

He sat up and got the remains of the sleep out of his eyes. 'I'd certainly like to accept the invitation, but I'm afraid I forgot to bring my swimming-trunks with me.'

'Does it matter?' she said. 'Nobody will arrest you here if you swim in the nude. I can guarantee that.'

'All the same—'

'Well,' she said, 'if it would embarrass you, you can wear those.' She pointed at a chair near the bed and he saw that a pair of blue trunks was lying on it and that another bathrobe was draped over the back. 'Now do get a move on. We're wasting time and it's a glorious morning.'

She showed no inclination to leave the room or even turn her back while he got out of the pyjamas and into the swimming-trunks; in fact she watched with considerable interest.

'There's one thing I'll say about you, Ray,' she remarked. 'You're very well made, in every respect.'

'I'm glad you think so,' Holden said.

'Oh, I do think so.' She moved closer to him and put a hand on his right arm, kneading the bicep muscle with her fingers. 'Mm! I guess you could give a good account of yourself in a rough-house.'

'I try to keep away from rough-houses. They tend to be bad for the health.'

She laughed. 'Don't tell me you've never been in a fight.'

'No, I won't tell you that; it wouldn't be true. But I never go looking for trouble.'

'You find it without looking, perhaps?'

'Sometimes.'

He pulled on the bathrobe and followed her to the door. When they came out of the room he looked for Morton or Katz but there was no sign of either of them; perhaps they had lost some sleep in the night and were making up for it now.

There was no one by the pool, either. Marcia dropped her bathrobe and went in off the springboard, making scarcely a splash. Holden saw that she had had practice; nobody dived like that first time round. She came up some distance away and turned to watch him. He made a clumsier entry into the water; he had never been an expert diver but he could swim well enough; he had raced a bit at one time.

When he came up with her she said: 'I wondered if you could swim. I see you can. Do you think you could beat me to the far end and back?'

She went off at a great rate without waiting for an answer, and she was ahead at the turn; but he passed her on the return stretch and she was breathing hard when she finished.

'You're pretty good,' she said, with frank admiration. 'But you knew that, of course.'

'I'm no world-beater.'

'Well, there aren't such a lot of them

148

around. But in my book you're good enough.'

When they came out of the pool they relaxed on padded sunbeds and soaked up the early morning warmth. Even with wet hair the girl looked gorgeous; she had the right kind of figure for the scarlet bikini; the kind you always saw in the glossy advertisements for Martinis or the Club Mediterranee or very flimsy, very expensive underwear.

'You're very nicely put together yourself,' Holden said.

She turned her head and smiled at him, obviously gratified. 'Well, thank you, Ray. I thought you'd never notice.'

'I noticed some time back. I only just got round to telling you.'

She was silent for a few moments, perhaps waiting for further compliments. But he made none, so she said: 'What do you think of this place?'

'I think it's fine. If the circumstances were somewhat different I could take quite a liking to it.'

'The circumstances could be different, you know.'

He gave her a questioning glance. 'What exactly are you implying?'

'How would you like a nice steady job, Ray?'

'You mean here?'

'Yes, here.'

'Are you suggesting I should do the kind of

job Morton and Katz do? Or did you have me earmarked for a stable-hand?'

'Neither.'

'What, then?'

'Oh, something quite different. More responsible. I'm sure I could persuade Uncle Charles to take you on. You're young, fit, educated, intelligent. You could be very useful in this organisation. The money would be good; you can be sure of that. There'd be a car—and other things maybe.'

He wondered whether the other things included Miss Marcia Brent. It seemed possible.

'Does it appeal to you, Ray?'

'No,' he said. 'I can't say it does.'

'Think about it. Don't turn it down out of hand.'

'I have thought about it, and the answer is still the same. No thanks.'

Her eyes clouded and her voice became sharper, less seductive. 'I guess I was wrong about the intelligence. Why are you turning it down?'

'Because, for one thing, I don't much like the kind of business your uncle is engaged in.'

'Well, that's fine, that is, coming from you. You're in that business yourself, aren't you?'

'I suppose you could say so. But I'm not very proud of it. It wasn't my idea; I got talked into it. And anyway it was to be just a one-off operation; I don't propose to make a career of

150

it.'

He thought she might try some more persuasion, but she did not. Perhaps her pride had been hurt by the bluntness of his refusal. If she had indeed been offering herself to him he could imagine how burned up she must be about it. She had probably expected him to jump at the chance, and no doubt there were a lot of men who, in his position, would have done so. Because when you took a good long look at that position you had to admit that it was none too happy a one, and it might be even less happy before the day was finished.

She stood up and pulled the bathrobe round her shoulders. 'Come with me,' she said. 'I've got something to show you. I think it will interest you.'

It was in a room in the basement. It was a long box resting on a table, and Holden's immediate thought when he saw it was that it looked remarkably like a coffin. There was a lid on it but it was not screwed down.

'Take a look inside,' Miss Brent said.

Holden got his fingers under the lid and lifted it. He peered into the box and was shocked by what he saw. Mr Gomez was lying there with his eyes closed, as though he might have been asleep. He looked very peaceful, neatly dressed in a dark suit and with no mark to show that he had sustained any injury. But he was not breathing, and from this sleep he would never wake.

Holden lowered the lid and turned away from the box that was indeed a coffin. He had a slight feeling of nausea; he rubbed the palms of his hands on the towelling material of the bathrobe he was wearing, as though to remove some contamination.

'So he's dead.'

'Yes. It was very sudden. Yesterday he was in the best of health. Today—as you see.'

'What's going to be done with him?'

'The interment,' Marcia said. 'will probably take place tonight. It will be a very private ceremony—just a few close friends but no relations.' She spoke with faint irony and a trace of amusement.

It amazed Holden that she could treat the killing of a man so lightly. For, there could be no doubt that Gomez had been killed; he had not simply expired from natural causes.

'Why?' he asked.

Her eyebrows lifted slightly. 'Do you really need to ask that? You must realise that he had been cheating us. It was he who put those two boys in the white Citroën on to you and Skene.'

'Can you be sure of that?'

'As sure as we need to be. As you heard, the same kind of thing had happened before, and we lost our shipments. That was why I was down in Mexico; I was doing a bit of investigating.'

'Oh, I see. And what did you find?'

'Enough. A hint here and there. It all pointed the same way. So we called Gomez up here for a consultation. We couldn't let it go on; we were paying for the cocaine and he was stealing it from us, our own agent. Do you think we could tolerate that?'

'We? You speak as if you were a partner in the business.'

'I am. A full partner. Uncle Charles relies a lot on me. We work things out together.'

'Is he married?'

'He was. Aunt Ellen died ten years ago. He has never remarried.'

'Perhaps he thinks a wife would be in the way.'

'Perhaps.'

'But you aren't?'

'Like I told you, I'm his right-hand girl.'

'I'm surprised that you tell me all this. Suppose I were to talk?'

'You won't, Ray,' she said.

The confidence with which she spoke made him uneasy. 'How can you be so sure?'

'Now don't look so unhappy,' she said. 'I just trust you, that's all. You're far too chivalrous to go telling tales about a lady.'

He knew she was laughing at him. She could laugh even with Gomez lying there in his coffin. It was the thought of the dead Señor Gomez that made him so uneasy, and all her assurances did not ease his mind. If they had not hesitated to remove their Mexican agent

153

on the merest suspicion of his double-dealing, why would they show any greater reluctance to eliminate a possible threat to their security? It might have been safer to have accepted Marcia's offer; she would have been on his side then. Now he could not be sure whether she was for or against him.

'Well now,' she said, 'if you've seen all you want to see down here I think we may as well go to breakfast.'

'I'm not hungry,' Holden said.

What he had seen and heard had most effectively robbed him of his appetite.

*　　　*　　　*

Skene rang through at the appointed time of eleven o'clock. Marcia came to tell Holden what arrangements had been made.

'The exchange is to take place at ten o'clock this evening. We'll be paying one hundred and twenty thousand dollars for the six bags of cocaine.'

'So you and Mr Hornsby decided to pay the asking price after all.'

'What else could we do? This way we recoup some of our losses; the other way we would have lost it all.'

'But you don't like doing it?'

'No, we don't like doing it. Who would? But we're realists and we don't let personal resentment come between us and the chance

154

of financial gain.'

He wondered whether she was being perfectly truthful. He would not have expected either her or Mr Hornsby to have given in quite so easily. So was there a catch in it somewhere? He looked into her eyes, searching for some hint of guile, but he could see none; she might have been the very personification of honesty. But he still had his doubts.

'Where is the exchange to take place?'

'Ah,' she said, 'that's where you come in. You're to direct us there and we're to take only one car. That's the arrangement.'

Holden thought about it. If it was being left to him to take the buyers to the rendezvous it had to be the old quarry again. The plan seemed to bear a strong resemblance to the earlier, ill-fated exchange with Benny the Fly and Finger Malone; even the timing was the same. He hoped that was not an omen.

'I expect,' Marcia said, 'they wanted to make sure we stuck to our side of the bargain and that we didn't leave you behind.'

'Yes, I expect so,' Holden said; and he wondered whether it had been Skene's idea or Belding's. He just hoped he would be able to find the way in the dark; but it ought to be no problem.

He was pretty much on edge for the rest of the day. Morton and Katz were keeping an eye on him again but he had no thoughts of

155

escaping; he would just have to co-operate in the arrangement that had been made and hope that everything went off smoothly.

There were a few black servants about the house but he saw very little of them; they seemed to have a genius for staying in the background. They were discreet, anonymous, self-effacing. He knew that it would have been useless to appeal to them for help; they knew too well where their advantage lay.

When the time of departure arrived he found that there were to be four of them and that they were to travel in a big black Cadillac. Besides himself there were Marcia and Morton and Katz. Mr Hornsby was not to be one of the party. It did not surprise him much; Hornsby was a director, not a doer.

'I shall be driving,' Marcia said. 'You'll sit in the front with me and tell me where to go. All right?'

'I suppose so.'

Morton was carrying a briefcase and he guessed the money was inside it. Katz had a brown holdall with a zip-fastener.

'What's that for?' Holden asked.

'We need something to put the cocaine in, don't we?' Marcia said.

'A bag that size? How much do you think there is?'

'Don't make a fuss,' she said. 'It's just a bag.'

He was not entirely happy about it. There was something odd about that bag and it bothered him. But everything bothered him; that was the way it was.

'Get in the car,' Marcia said.

He got into the front passenger seat and Morton and Katz piled into the back. Having the two of them behind him made his nape crawl a bit; but they were not going to shoot him, he could be sure of that; at least not before he had guided them to the rendezvous.

When they drove past the Red Ace garage the place looked absolutely dead; there was not a light showing.

'What do you suppose Mr Crane is doing?' Holden said.

'What Crane is doing is none of your business,' Marcia answered a trifle sharply. 'You'd do well to forget about him.'

'I'll be only too happy to. I just wondered how much he knows about what goes on.'

'He knows just as much as he needs to know and no more.'

'And that isn't a lot, I imagine.'

'You can imagine what you like,' she said.

There was rather more life in Briggsville; there was even a police car on the prowl but the men in it were not looking for a black Cadillac. Marcia drove through the town and they left the welcome sign behind.

When it came to the point he remembered the way perfectly. It was precisely five minutes to ten when they came to the dirt road.

'Turn right here,' he said, 'and take it slowly

157

because this road is bad.'

Marcia followed his instructions and the headlights bored a tunnel through the darkness under the trees. A little while later they reached the quarry and he could see the bus parked, dark and silent, on the right, with the green Ford not far away from it. There was a light showing in the open doorway of the hut.

'You'd better stop here,' he said. 'And switch off the headlights.'

She did so. The Cadillac had come to a halt some twenty or thirty yards from the hut and he saw Belding appear in the doorway. There was no sign of Skene or any of the girls.

'Now what?' Holden said. 'Do you want me to go and talk to him?'

Belding was still standing in the doorway and not making any move; he seemed to be waiting for them to come to him.

'No,' Marcia said. 'You and I wait here. Morton and Katz will make the exchange.'

They were already getting out of the car, Morton with the briefcase and Katz with the holdall. They began to walk quite slowly towards the hut. He saw Belding's mouth working, as though he were saying something to the two men, but the words were not audible at that distance.

Morton and Katz were about five yards from the hut when they came to a halt, and Katz put the holdall on the ground. Holden could see Katz sliding back the zip-fastener

158

and reaching into the bag.

He spoke to Marcia. 'What the devil is he doing with that holdall?'

'You'll see,' she said; and he thought he detected a note of suppressed excitement in her voice.

Katz's hand came out of the holdall, and Holden did see. There was a submachine-gun in it. He saw Katz cock the gun and he even caught the metallic snick as he did so. And then Katz was firing the gun, and Belding was falling back inside the hut with a lot of holes in his chest.

Holden made a move to open the door on his side and get out of the car; he had a hazy idea of going to Belding's aid, though there would have been no sense in it, because Hank was surely dead with all that metal in him and no one on earth could help him now. But in any case he never got as far as doing anything of the kind, because Marcia Brent said something to him.

She said: 'Stop right there, Ray.'

And as if to emphasise the fact that she meant him to obey her she pressed something hard into his side, and when he looked down to see what it was he discovered that she was holding a small automatic pistol in her hand.

CHAPTER TWELVE

HELL OF A DAY

'You're not going any place,' she said. 'Not until Morton and Katz have done their job.'

Holden looked towards the hut and saw that the two men had gone inside, stepping over Belding's dead body. He could guess what they were looking for and he saw all too clearly that there had never been any intention of handing over any money for the cocaine. The briefcase had been no more than a blind; there had been nothing in it, not even stage money; he could see it now where Morton had thrown it to the ground.

'You cheated,' he said.

'We were cheated first,' Marcia said. 'You surely didn't expect we were going to take it lying down, that we were going to hand out one hundred and twenty thousand dollars as easily as that.'

He had never really believed it; it would have been too simple. But he had never suspected that Hornsby and his niece would choose such a ruthless and bloody way as this to gain their ends. Morton and Katz had obviously come with orders to shoot and kill without asking questions.

Yet there had been no more shots fired

160

after the initial burst that had killed Belding. So it looked as if they had not found Skene inside the hut. They were still in there and he wondered what they could be doing; all they needed to do was to pick up the cocaine and come out again. So what was keeping them?

And then he saw Skene appear from the darkness and he guessed that the plan had been much as before, when Sabata and Malone had come: Belding would make the swap and Skene would wait outside in case there was any slip-up. But this time there had been more than a slip-up; this time it had not worked out the same way, because these men had come shooting. Now Skene had real trouble on his hands.

But he had a gun; he had the automatic that had been Malone's; Holden could see it in his hand as he came out of the shadows and ran with a curious bounding stride towards the hut. He stopped when he came to the doorway and crouched slightly, holding the gun with both hands.

He made a mistake then; he should have started firing at once, the way Katz had done; but he gave a shout. Holden was unable to see the other two men but he could imagine them swinging round to face the doorway when Skene shouted, and seeing him there, crouched, with the automatic in his hands. Skene fired then and somebody gave a cry of pain; but he had left it too late; the submachine-gun stuttered again and he fell over and lay where he had fallen.

Katz came out of the hut with the gun in his hands. He looked down at Skene and kicked him and then he began walking towards the Cadillac. Morton came out, too, and followed him. Morton's left arm was hanging limply and there was blood dripping from the hand, so there was no doubt about who had uttered the cry of pain.

Katz reached the car first. Marcia had the window down on her side and he spoke through it. He sounded angry and frustrated.

'They played a trick on us. They didn't have the stuff in the hut.'

'You looked for it?'

'You bet we looked for it. Ain't no way it can be in there. And now Joe's bin hit.'

The girl glanced at Morton. 'How bad is it?'

'Bad enough,' Morton said, gasping a little. 'The bastard! I'd like to—'

'He's dead,' Katz said. 'Forget him.'

Marcia looked at Holden and her voice was hard. 'Where's the cocaine?'

'How would I know?' Holden said. 'I haven't been here, have I? They could have hidden it anywhere. Obviously they didn't trust you. I wonder why.'

She ignored the jibe. 'You, Katz, go search that bus. Maybe it's in there.'

'Wait,' Holden said. 'The girls are in there.'

It was a wonder to him that they had not come

162

out when the shooting started; but perhaps they had been too scared.

Katz did not appear to have heard him; he was already on his way.

'What girls?' Marcia asked.

'The three who were travelling with us.'

'Oh,' she said, with a sneer, 'so you've been well provided for. You didn't tell me about the female company.'

'It was none of your damned business.'

He saw that Katz was getting near the bus; but he was still about a dozen yards away from it when two of the girls came out and started running. Holden could not tell which two they were. Katz shouted at them to stop but they kept going; they were probably in a panic and had only one thought—to get away.

Katz did not bother to shout again; he lifted the submachine-gun and mowed them down.

'The swine!' Holden said. 'The stinking, bloody, murdering swine!'

He opened the door of the car and got one foot out.

'Stay where you are,' Marcia said; and she rammed the muzzle of the pistol viciously into his ribs.

He turned his head and snarled at her: 'Damn you, you bitch!' He was too angry to heed the gun in his side. He swung his clenched fist back-handed and struck her on the mouth. She gave a cry and fell back against the other door, the pistol going off in her

163

hand.

He felt a searing pain just below the bottom rib on his left side as the bullet gouged its way through the flesh; but he had been hitting her as she pressed the trigger and it had spoiled her aim. For the moment she seemed to be dazed and he took the opportunity to get out of the car. But then he saw Morton, and Morton had a pistol in his right hand. His left arm was still hanging limply and he was swaying a bit, as though his legs could scarcely support him, but he raised the pistol and aimed it at Holden; and though his gun-arm was none too steady he was a menace all the same.

'Get back,' he said.

Holden scarcely heard him; he was not listening. He saw Morton simply as an obstacle which had to be brushed aside and he gave no thought to the gun; he just went straight at the man and kicked him in the groin. He heard the crack of the pistol and the bullet might have been close but it passed by without hitting him. Morton gave a scream and fell to the ground, writhing in agony. Holden kicked him on the chin and knocked him cold.

His left side was numb but he could feel the blood trickling down his leg. He glanced across to where the girls were lying and he could see no movement there; it was pretty certain that they were dead. He wondered about the third one and he made a move towards the bus. But

164

then he saw Katz and changed his mind.

Katz was coming towards him with the submachine-gun. He had it raised but he was not firing, and that might have been because the car was directly behind Holden and he was afraid of hitting it and perhaps putting a bullet into Miss Brent. Holden saw very clearly that there was no future in going to meet Katz, however much he might wish to smash the man's face with his clenched fist; Katz had too much fire-power and he had none. The only sensible thing to do was to get away from there fast, and he did it.

He got round to the other side of the car and began to run. He ran towards the dirt road and he could hear Katz yelling to him to stop. He glanced back and saw Katz just coming round the car about thirty yards behind him. Katz fired a burst from the submachine-gun but he did it running and the bullets scattered stones and dust but did no harm.

Holden was on the road then and moving fast. He ran on for another fifty yards and then got off the road and into the trees. It was just about pitch-dark in there and he went plunging blindly on through the undergrowth, bumping into things and feeling low-hanging branches and tendrils brushing him as he went past. Something tripped him and he fell headlong into a shallow hole. His chest was burning and he just lay there, listening.

At first he could hear nothing save the

165

rustling of leaves in the light breeze but then his ears caught the sound of someone forcing a way through the undergrowth and it was certain that it could only be Katz searching for him. He felt an urge to get up and start running again but reason told him that if he stayed where he was there was a good chance that Katz would not find him; it was utterly dark where he was lying and the hunter obviously had no torch.

Five or ten minutes passed with Katz stumbling around and coming uncomfortably close at times; and he even fired a few bursts from the submachine-gun in his frustration. But finally he must have decided to abandon the search, for the sound of his movements died away and once again there was only the rustling of the leaves.

Holden remained where he was for a while after that, in case Katz was being cunning and had stopped moving around in the hope that the fugitive might reveal his whereabouts. But finally he came to the conclusion that Katz really had gone away, and he got out of the hole and made his way with some difficulty out of the trees and round the rim of the quarry until he reached a point from which he could look down into it. Lying on his chest and peering over the edge, he was able to discern Marcia Brent standing by the Cadillac, so apparently she had recovered somewhat from the blow he had given her. He could see neither of the men and he surmised that Morton, having regained consciousness, had got himself into the car and was nursing his wounds. But where was Katz?

Then he noticed that the lights were on in the bus and a moment later he saw Katz come out of it, dragging the third girl with him and carrying the submachine-gun in his free hand. Which of the girls it was Holden could still not be certain but she must have been hiding in the bus and hoping to remain undiscovered. And such hope must always have been a faint one, but at least Katz had not shot her out of hand, so perhaps he had been given orders to take her alive. Marcia would have known there was one girl remaining, because Holden himself had told her that there were three of them, and maybe she wanted this last one as a hostage.

Katz hauled the girl across to the Cadillac and Marcia opened one of the rear doors and they pushed her inside. Then Katz went back to the bus. He was inside for quite a while, no doubt searching for the cocaine. Holden lay on the ground and shivered in the cool night air. His side was beginning to burn now that the initial numbness was wearing off, and he wondered how much blood he had lost.

Then he saw Katz come out of the bus and walk over to the green Ford. The doors were not locked and he switched on the interior light so that he could be clearly seen searching around inside. He looked in the boot and under the bonnet but found nothing to his purpose. Finally he gave up and walked back to the Cadillac.

He and Miss Brent went into a huddle and Holden guessed they were none too pleased with the way things had gone. Watching them from a distance and unable to hear a word they were saying, he nevertheless got the impression that they were two very angry persons. One thing was certain: the girl they had taken out of the bus had not been able to tell them what they would have liked to know, so it was a fairly safe bet that she did not know, either. She would have been far too frightened to hold that information back if she had been able to give it.

Marcia and Katz ended their discussion after a minute or two and got into the Cadillac, this time with Katz at the wheel. Perhaps Miss Brent was still feeling somewhat under the weather from the effect of being punched on the mouth and did not feel like driving.

Holden watched them drive away and then made his way back to the dirt road and into the quarry. He walked over to where the two girls were lying and saw that they were Rosita and Cecile. He felt angry and sad to see those poor bloodstained bodies but there was a sense of relief also; he had feared that one of them might have been Ruth Belding but he knew now that she at least was still alive.

Somehow he had to make sure she stayed that way.

He walked to the hut and the light from the lantern inside revealed the bodies of the two men. He went into the hut and with a certain amount of pain and effort succeeded in pulling Belding away from the door. He went outside and dragged Skene in and laid him beside the other man. One after the other he carried the dead girls into the hut and then he fetched some sheets from the bus to cover the bodies. He took the lantern away and closed the hut door behind him and left them there in the darkness. It had been a wretched job to do and he was sick afterwards and felt like death himself.

Nevertheless, he got a spade from the bus and took it with the lantern to the other side of the quarry where there was a hollow at the foot of the cliff like a small cave. He dug some earth away and found the biscuit-tin with the bags of cocaine inside where they had buried it. It had been Belding's suggestion to put it there after the fiasco with Sabata and Malone, and they had said nothing to the girls about it. That, too, had been Belding's idea and in view of what had subsequently happened it almost seemed as though he had had some presentiment of what was to come. Though of course no one, not even he, could possibly have foreseen such carnage as had taken place. He had said at the outset that it would be

169

dangerous to go to Mr Bradley and, though Bradley had proved to be a non-existent person, he could not have been more correct in his estimation of the risk.

Well, he was dead now, and Skene was dead, and two of the girls were dead; which was a hell of a price to pay for the hope of a fistful of dollars. If it had not been for the surviving girl Holden would have opened the bags of cocaine and scattered the contents in the dirt. But he had to keep them intact for just a while yet; they were all he had to bargain with.

He went back to the bus, carrying the tin with him; and he put the tin on one of the seats and looked down at his left side. There were two holes in his shirt where the bullet had gone in and come out and there was a big red stain where the blood had come through. The left trouser-leg was soaked too and the blood had dripped on to his shoe and into it, so that his foot felt damp and sticky. He was in the devil of a state and feeling sick again, and his legs felt like boiled spaghetti. He wanted to lie down but there were things to do.

He went to the back of the bus where the toilet was and he stripped off all his clothes and tried to get a look at himself in the mirror. All he could see in the glass looked bad and, when he looked down at the wound in his side, that looked bad, too. He ran some water into the wash-bowl and began to wash away the blood. He felt the sting of the cold water on the gash in his side and where the blood had clotted it opened up and began to bleed again.

But it was not as bad as he had feared, though bad enough to make him have some very unfriendly thoughts about Marcia Brent. It was a shallow wound about four inches long; a fraction of an inch higher and the bullet would have shattered the bottom rib, and even as it was there was a possibility that it had chipped it; he could feel some pain in that part when he breathed in deeply, or even not so deeply. So maybe he had better stop breathing deeply. Maybe he was lucky to be breathing at all.

When he had cleaned himself up as well as he could he opened the first-aid kit and found some antiseptic, which he dabbed on the wound. The kit was not very comprehensive but there were some packets of lint from which he made a dressing for the wound and stuck it on with some of the adhesive tape he had bought in Nuevo Laredo for Rosita to fix the bags of cocaine to her body. Well, she would never do that again. It would have been better for her if she had stayed on with her rich American rancher; and maybe she would have done so if the man's wife had not come back. In a way it might be said that that woman caused her death without even knowing it. Poor little Rosita, who had been so full of life. And poor little Cecile, too, if it came to that.

Belding and Skene had asked for what they had got; but the girls, no; never the girls. They had been innocent victims.

By the time he had finished dressing the wound it was getting on for midnight and he decided to try to get some sleep. He doubted whether it would be possible but he put the lights out and crawled into one of the bunks and lay on his back. The wound throbbed but did not pain him too much, and he was so dead tired that, even after all that had happened, in a very little while he was asleep.

It had been a hell of a day; it really had been one hell of a day.

CHAPTER THIRTEEN

DISTURBANCE

He awoke in the half-light of early morning with a dry mouth and no great feeling of having been much refreshed by sleep. It took a few moments for the complete memory of what had happened the previous day to make its way into his brain; and when it did it was scarcely something to be welcomed with a sense of rapturous joy.

He was immediately aware of the injury that had been inflicted on him. He pushed back the blanket and pulled himself up in the bunk in

172

order to take a look at the dressing. He was not terribly happy with what he saw; blood had soaked through the lint and it looked a mess. But the blood had dried and it seemed that the wound was no longer bleeding. He came to the conclusion that the best course would be to leave the dressing in place; it would be hell getting it off, anyway, and might cause the gash to open up and start bleeding again.

There seemed to have been a certain amount of stiffening in that part of his body and when he moved he was getting more of the pain than he had before going to sleep; but he supposed that was natural. The bottom rib made him unhappily aware of its presence even when he was not breathing very deeply, and all the flesh in the region of the injury had taken on something of the colour of an apple that was starting to go rotten. All in all, he was not in the best of shape for a man who had so many things waiting for him to do.

With some difficulty and no little discomfort he got off the bunk and found some clean clothes and dressed himself. He had a shave and made some strong coffee in the little kitchen and when he had soaked up a cup of the hot liquid he began to feel rather more like a real live human being. He fried some bacon and opened a tin of beans and ate a pretty good breakfast. And then he drank some more coffee and gave a bit of thought to the situation.

It was not good, that was certain. It was broad daylight now and the sun was beginning to put some warmth into the air. He looked through the windows of the old bus and he could see the green Ford and the hut in which the four bodies were lying, and further away the fall of earth covering the grave of those other two bodies. It amazed him that nobody else had come to the quarry. So much had taken place there—stabbing, shooting and general mayhem—that it hardly seemed credible that no one should have come to investigate. But of course there was not a house or other building anywhere near the place and it was quite possible that weeks or even months passed by without a single person visiting it.

He got himself out of the bus and walked across to the Ford. The keys were in it, which was something in his favour and maybe a good omen for what the rest of the day might have in store for him. Not that he felt like putting much faith in that kind of omen; everything would probably go wrong; it had all gone wrong so far, so why should there be any change now?

He checked the petrol and found that the tank was a trifle under half-full. He had a powerful urge to take the car and get to hell out of there. He had no idea where he would go, but what did it matter as long as it was somewhere miles from this place? He got into

174

the driving-seat and started the engine; but then he stopped it again, because this was something he could not clear up by running away; there was the girl to think about—Ruth Belding. What kind of a louse would he be if he just took to his heels and left her to manage as best she could?

He went back to the bus and got the biscuit-tin and took it to the car. He put it in the boot and covered it with a piece of sacking that was in there and locked the lid. As he was returning to the bus he saw the pistol that Skene had used still lying where he had dropped it. He walked over to it and picked it up and carried it to the bus.

It was getting on for ten o'clock when he took the Ford out of the quarry. He drove to Briggsville and found a public telephone and dialled Hornsby's number.

It was Marcia Brent who answered and judging by the sound of her voice coming over the wire he would have said she was not in the best of tempers.

'This is Ray Holden,' he said.

'Oh,' she said, 'so you're still around.'

'Yes, I'm still around. I'd like to say I'm in the best of health but it wouldn't be true. I've got a pretty nasty pain under the ribs.'

'Too bad,' she said; and she was not dishing out any sympathy as far as he could detect. He was certainly not her number one favourite man any longer. Maybe he had never really been that but for a time it had seemed as though she were angling for him.

'Where are you?' she asked.

'Never mind where I am. Tell me about Miss Belding.'

'What do you want to know?'

'Is she all right?'

'She's in good shape.'

'But you're not letting her go?'

'No.'

'I'll make a bargain with you.'

'What kind of bargain?'

'You let her go free and I'll give you what you didn't get last night.'

'So you've got it?'

'Yes.'

'Where was it hidden?'

'It doesn't matter where it was hidden. Is it a deal?'

'Wait a minute,' she said.

He guessed she had gone to speak to her uncle, and half a minute later Hornsby himself came on the line.

'Are you there, Holden?'

'I'm here.'

'It's a deal,' Hornsby said. 'You bring the stuff and the girl is free to go. But no tricks. That way you could get hurt.'

'I am already hurt and I've run out of tricks,' Holden said. 'I'll be at your place this evening. Nine o'clock.'

'Why so late? Why not come straightaway?

176

Get it over with.'

'I can't do that.'

'You aren't setting something up, are you?' Hornsby sounded suspicious.

'No, I'm not setting anything up. You can trust me.'

'I hope so. I just hope so.'

'See you tonight, then,' Holden said and rang off.

He did not leave the call-box at once but dialled another number, and when he got an answer from the other end of the line he said: 'My name is Ray Holden. Now listen carefully to what I'm going to say, and for God's sake don't interrupt because it's important. Okay?'

'Okay, shoot,' the voice in his ear said.

He spoke his piece and there was a slight pause.

'Have you got that?' he asked.

'Is this on the level?' the voice said; and there was a lot of doubt in the tone. Maybe that was only to be expected.

'It's on the level. And you'd better believe it.'

'Where are you calling from?'

'Never mind where I'm calling from,' Holden said. 'Just do what I've asked.'

He rang off then and got out of the call-box and walked back to the car. He hoped to God they did believe it, because otherwise he would be in bad trouble. He was in trouble anyway but he could be in worse. So he hoped they

177

believed him and would do what he had asked; but he could not be sure they would; he could be sure of nothing except the trouble.

He wondered whether it would be safe to go back to the quarry. Hornsby and Marcia might figure he would be holed up there and they might have ideas of coming out and taking the cocaine from him. But it was unlikely. Why would they bother when they knew he was coming to them? And of course Morton was probably in rather a bad way and not likely to be taking much part in any activity. The best place for him would be a hospital but somehow Holden could not quite imagine Hornsby letting Morton go into hospital with a bullet wound; that kind of thing was liable to cause talk. Maybe they had had a doctor out to the ranch to see to him—one who, at a price, could be relied on to do his job and keep his mouth shut.

When Holden got back to the car he was feeling bad; he ought to have been in hospital himself, or at least to have had somebody look at his wound. But that was out of the question for the present. Later perhaps. But who knew just what would happen later?

He drove back to the quarry and it was still deserted. He locked the car and got into the bus and lay down for a while. A little after noon he opened a tin of corned beef and made some sandwiches. He ate the sandwiches and washed them down with more strong coffee.

He examined the pistol. It was a compact weapon—a .32 calibre Walther, handy for the pocket. There was still a round in the chamber and he left it there with the safety-catch on. The clip had six rounds left in it. Skene had managed to fire just the one shot and that was the one that had smashed Morton's arm. He hoped he himself would have no cause to use the gun at all but that was something else he could not be sure about.

It was warm in the bus, even with the windows open. He had nearly eight more hours to kill before his appointment at the Hornsby ranch, and there was nothing to do but hang around and wait for the time to pass. There were some books in the bus and he tried to put in some reading; but his mind would not concentrate on the print and he gave it up. His head was aching slightly and he wondered whether he had a touch of fever. He made another rummage in the medicine-chest and came up with a bottle of aspirins. He swallowed a couple and lay down again on the bunk. He closed his eyes and tried not to think about all the problems that were lined up ahead of him. He tried to empty his mind completely and leave it a perfect vacuum; but he had never been much good at that kind of thing and it failed to work now; the stuff that was in there stayed in and went churning round and round as merrily as ever. And the aspirins were not doing a lot for his aches and pains, either.

Nevertheless, he must have dozed off after a time, for suddenly he was brought back to full consciousness by the devil of a racket going on outside. He eased himself out of the bunk and looked through one of the side windows, and what he saw was not calculated to do much for his peace of mind.

There were three large, powerful motor-cycles careering round and round the quarry, and sitting on the bikes were three men in black boots, black breeches, black leather jackets and black crash-helmets. Attached to the jackets was a considerable amount of glinting hardware—chains, studs, badges and various other embellishments; their backs were adorned with representations of death's-heads picked out in white luminous paint and on the helmets were blood-red swastikas.

Holden drew back from the window in order not to be seen. He hoped that the motor-cyclists would soon grow tired of riding round the quarry and would go away; but he was to be disappointed. After about ten minutes of the circling exercise they all pulled up a few yards from the hut, got off the machines, removed their helmets and lit cigarettes. They all had close-cropped hair and he could see that they were young. There was a kind of swagger about them; they talked in loud voices and laughed a good deal.

Holden was on tenterhooks. He feared they

180

might take it into their heads to look inside the hut; and if they did that they would find the dead bodies and he would be in more trouble. This was a complication he had neither foreseen nor wanted.

Then one of the men strolled over to the Ford. It seemed to interest him; he peered in through the windows and tried the doors. Holden was thankful he had locked the car and taken the keys; the man might have had the idea of doing a bit of joy-riding. As it was, he was frustrated by the locked doors. But he did not give up easily; Holden saw him take a large clasp-knife from his pocket and start on what looked like a job of lock-picking.

It was time to forget about keeping a low profile. Holden picked up the pistol, stowed it in his pocket and stepped down from the bus.

'You can stop that,' he said.

The man who was working on the car door turned and looked at him. He had a round, snub-nosed face and a mass of acne like eruptions on the surface of a dead planet.

'You talkin' to me?' he asked.

'That's right,' Holden said. 'What do you think you're doing to my car?'

'Oh, so it's your car, is it? You own the bus, too? If it is a bus.'

'It belongs to my friends.'

'I don't see no friends.'

'They're asleep.'

'At this time of day?'

'We were travelling most of the night. We're tired. Maybe you wouldn't mind leaving now so that we can have some peace and quiet.'

The man turned and shouted to the other two: 'Hear that, you guys? Man wants us to go. Says we're disturbing the peace.'

They all laughed.

'All right,' Holden said. 'So it's a big joke. All right.'

The man with the acne went back to his motor-cycle and started the engine. Holden thought perhaps he was being more reasonable than had seemed likely and actually intended leaving; but he had not put his helmet on and all he did was make a lot of noise with the engine while the others lounged against the hut, watching him, listening to the crackle of the exhaust, smoking and grinning.

Holden walked across to the hut. The man with acne switched off the engine of the motor-cycle and joined the others. He was standing almost in the doorway of the hut.

Holden said: 'I'd be much obliged if you would go away. My friends really are trying to get some sleep.'

'Know what I think?' the man said. 'I think you don't have no friends. I think you're all alone in the world.' He appealed to his companions. 'Would you say he looks like a guy that'd have friends? Honest now, would you?'

'Seems like a loner to me,' one of the others

182

said. He was perhaps twenty years old and there was a vicious look about him. He had squinting eyes and a thin mouth. 'See here, feller,' he said, addressing Holden, 'you got no rights to tell us to go. This place don't belong to you. Mebbe we'll stay here all night. Sleep in this here little ol' log cabin.'

'You won't do that,' Holden said, perhaps a shade too quickly.

'Why not? You own that, too?'

'No, but—'

The idea of sleeping in the hut seemed to catch on, perhaps because they could see it bothered Holden. The third man lifted the catch of the door and pushed it open a little way. Holden took a couple of steps forward and put a hand on his shoulder, trying to pull him back.

'Don't go in there.'

'Take your goddam hand offa me,' the man said.

'No. I'm telling you, you can't go in there.'

'Aw, shit!' The man swung his right arm, hitting Holden on the side of the neck. 'Outa the way, creep.'

Holden staggered. They were all jostling him. One of them pushed him in the chest, another put out a foot and tripped him, and he fell awkwardly to the ground with a sudden agonising pain in his injured side. He gave an involuntary cry and they all laughed again. One of them kicked him. The others were already going into the hut. The one who had delivered the kick followed them in.

Holden struggled to his feet and hauled the gun out of his pocket. He went to the door of the hut but he was too late; they had pulled the sheets aside and were staring at the four dead bodies.

'Oh, Jeeze!' the one with the acne said in a low, scared voice. 'Four stiffs!' He dropped the sheet he was holding and shrank back, white-faced, his lips trembling.

The others, too, retreated from the blood-stained corpses, still staring at them in horror. None of them looked so tough now; the swagger had gone out of them. In the presence of so much violent death they had lost their nerve.

Holden stood in the doorway with the gun in his hand. 'I told you not to go in.'

They turned and looked at him, at the gun.

'He's crazy,' one of them muttered. 'He's a crazy killer.' He looked as though he would have liked to make a run for it but the man with the gun was blocking the only way out. 'Don't shoot, mister. Don't shoot. We won't say nothin'.'

'I told you not to disturb my friends,' Holden said. 'But you wouldn't listen.'

He was still getting a lot of pain from his wound and it made him grimace. The grimace must have seemed like a grin of rage or madness to the men with the death's-heads on

184

their backs. They were not taunting him now; not laughing, either.

'Why don't you go?' Holden said. He was oblivious of the fact that he was standing in the way. He could not understand why they made no move. 'Do you want me to kill you? Is that what you want?'

'No, mister, no! Don't do that! Don't shoot!'

'Then go, damn you! Go!'

It occurred to him then to step back out of the doorway. They came out with a rush. They could not get to their bikes fast enough. They got the engines started and rammed the helmets on their heads and were away, loose stones spraying from the tyres, exhausts snarling defiance. There was no circling the quarry this time; they headed straight for the dirt road and were gone.

Holden put the pistol back in his pocket and went into the hut and replaced the covering on the disfigured bodies. He tried not to look at them but it was as though his eyes were drawn to the grisly sight. He shuddered and let the sheets fall soundlessly back upon the two men and the two young women who had loved them.

He went out of the hut and closed the door. There was no sound of motor-cycle engines now to disturb the peace of the quarry; it was all very quiet. The coming of the three black-clad men had introduced a further complication. Would they, he wondered, go to the police? Perhaps. But he did not think so; characters of that sort would surely prefer not to become involved; their one aim would be to get away. Nevertheless, he could not be certain; they might act like honest citizens for once. So he had to leave now; he could not wait any longer; it was not safe.

He returned to the bus and began to pack his bag. It did not take long. He carried the bag to the car and stowed away the Walther pistol. He started the engine and drove out of the quarry.

CHAPTER FOURTEEN

KILLING TIME

He drove at a moderate speed; he had any amount of time and there was no need for haste. What he had to find was some place where he could wait until late evening, the hour of his appointment at the Hornsby ranch.

When he had put about ten miles between himself and the old quarry he kept an eye open for a minor road. It was not long before he saw a likely one branching off to the left, and he took the car on to it and drove slowly, looking about him for a suitable spot in which to park.

The place he eventually chose was in among

some trees; it was shady, peaceful and out of sight of any building. Now and then a car went past on the road but there was no great amount of traffic and he doubted whether he could have found anywhere more suited to his purpose—the killing of time.

He sat in the car and waited. Half an hour passed and his side was hurting; it seemed impossible to find any position which would ease the grumbling pain of the wound. It had been bleeding again after his encounter with the motor-cycle yobs, and some of the blood had soaked through his shirt. Looking down, he could see the dark stain of it just above the waistband of his trousers.

At the end of an hour of sitting there he decided to get out of the car and lie down on the grass. He lay on his back with his gaberdine zipper jacket folded to serve as a pillow, and it was an improvement on sitting in the car. The pain eased a little. He closed his eyes; he was still feeling tired and after a while he dozed off.

When he opened his eyes there was a man staring down at him. From his position on the ground it seemed to Holden that the man was extraordinarily tall and thin. His head appeared curiously like that of a bird of prey; the eyes singularly bright, the nose aquiline and predatory, the chin receding into a long wrinkled neck.

'Are you all right?' the man asked. He was

187

dressed in a check shirt with the sleeves rolled up to the elbows, blue denim trousers and a pair of scuffed shoes with no polish on them. He had a wheezy kind of voice, rather high-pitched. He looked old.

'I'm all right,' Holden said.

'You got blood on your shirt,' the man said. He was not too old to recognise blood when he saw it.

'Yes.'

'How come?'

'I was using a knife. I cut myself.'

'In the gut? Mighty funny place to cut yourself with a knife; 'less you was tryin' to commit harry-karry.' He went off into a croaking laugh that seemed to rattle his old bones.

'Don't let it bother you.'

'Son,' the old man said, 'it don't bother me none. You's the one should be bothered.'

Holden raised himself into a sitting posture and it was as though something were being torn apart under his left ribs. He gasped with the pain of it and his head swam for a moment.

'You don't look all that cracky to me,' the man said. 'Look, son, I got me a little place a mite down the road. You could go there, rest up some, mebbe let me get a doctor.'

'No,' Holden said. 'No doctor.'

'Okay; it's your say-so. Come all the same. Mebbe you could use a bite to eat. Won't cost you nothin'. My name's Skillimore.'

Holden thought about it. It might be a good offer to accept. At Skillimore's place he could put the car away where it would attract no unwelcome attention, and he could rest until evening.

'Is anyone else there?' he asked.

Skillimore shook his head. 'Nary a one. I live by meself. Nobody's going to bother you.'

Holden wondered why Skillimore was being so helpful. What was there in it for him? Well, perhaps he was simply a good Samaritan who believed in giving a helping hand to his fellow-man whenever he saw the chance. Or maybe he was just a lonely old man who craved a bit of human company.

'My name is Roberts,' Holden said. 'And thank you for the invitation. I'll be glad to accept your hospitality.'

He started to get up. Skillimore stretched out a hand to help him. It felt like a bundle of bones in a thin leather bag. But the old man was stronger than he looked; he had a firm grip and a pretty solid pull.

They got into the car and Holden backed it on to the road. Skillimore's place was no more than a hundred yards away; they turned a corner and there it was, a long wooden bungalow standing well back from the road in a jungle that might once have been a garden.

'Used to have me a little truck-farm one time,' Skillimore said. 'Made money, too. Then m' wife died an' I got to be old, so I sold

189

the land and kept the house. I manage. Folks say I oughta go into a home for senior citizens, but the hell with that. Git in one o' them places an' you might's well be dead.'

'I think you're right,' Holden said. He was beginning to like Skillimore; the old man certainly had spirit.

There was a pick-up truck standing in an open-fronted shed at one side of the bungalow, dented and rusty; it looked as though it had done a load of work in its time. Holden stopped the Ford in front of the shed.

'You drive the pick-up?'

'Sure do,' Skillimore said. 'When I got places to go. How else'd I get there?'

Holden thought the vehicle was a fit match for its owner. The bungalow, too; it had not been painted in years and some of the wood was rotting; there were a few shingles missing from the roof; one of the windows was broken and had been repaired with polythene sheeting.

They went round to the back. There was a porch with two steps leading up to it.

'Mind how you go,' Skillimore warned. 'That top step ain't as good as it might be.'

The step creaked as Holden set his foot on it, but it bore his weight. A door opening off the back porch gave access to a kitchen which looked as though it might be waiting for the long-departed Mrs Skillimore to return and do something about it. It was in a mess; there

190

were dirty dishes, dirty saucepans, dirty cutlery; everything seemed to have acquired a protective coating of grease; there were empty, unwashed tins lying around gathering dust and flies; there was some scummy water in the sink with half-submerged utensils like a scuttled battle fleet.

Skillimore cleared a space on the plain wooden table which bore the traces of his last meal, and possibly of several earlier meals.

'You like me to fry some ham 'n' eggs?'

'No,' Holden said. 'Thanks all the same, but I'm not really hungry.' Skillimore's kitchen had effectively killed any appetite he might have had.

'You sure? Wouldn't be no bother.'

'Don't trouble,' Holden said. 'If I could just rest for a while—'

'Sure, sure. But I still reckon you should have a doctor.'

'There's no need. I'll be all right.'

'Okay, if that's the way you want it. Jus' come alonga me.'

Skillimore led the way to a bedroom. It must have been the one he used. The bed had not been made but he straightened the quilt with a few sharp tugs of the hand. Then he drew a curtain across the window, putting the room in shadow.

'Anythin' else you want 'fore I go?'

'Nothing, thank you,' Holden said.

'I'll leave you, then.'

Skillimore went out of the room and closed the door. Holden kicked off his shoes and lay down on the bed. It was warm in the room and there was a stale odour of human occupation which was not altogether pleasant. He ignored the odour and closed his eyes.

He did not sleep; he just lay there waiting for the minutes to tick away. After a quarter of an hour, or it might have been more, he began to wonder what Skillimore was doing. And then he gradually became uneasy; perhaps he ought not to have been so trusting. What did he know about Skillimore? Nothing, apart from what the man had told him; which was not much. So maybe he had better not lie there any longer; maybe he had better go and see just exactly what the old man was doing.

He eased himself off the bed and with some protest from his injured side he got his shoes on again. He opened the door softly and as soon as he had it open he could hear Skillimore's voice coming from somewhere not far away. There was a narrow passage outside the bedroom, leading to a cramped lobby and the front door. He could not see Skillimore but he guessed that he was in this lobby and he wondered who the old man was talking to. If he had a visitor it might be the wrong kind and might be dangerous.

Holden tiptoed down the passage and peeped into the lobby and saw that there was no one with Skillimore. But things could hardly have been worse if there had been. Skillimore was standing with his back towards Holden and he was speaking into a telephone. There was a small table which the telephone stood on, and on the table was lying the Walther self-loading pistol. It gave him quite a jolt to see it, but he got more of a jolt when he heard what Skillimore was saying.

'That's right. Like I said he's bin wounded in the gut. He's restin' on my bed right now, but I guess he'll git movin' 'fore long, so don't waste more time than you can help. He had a gun in the car, but I got it now, a little fancy pistol. And there's a tin in the trunk with some plastic bags in it. Drugs, I guess. The car's a green Ford . . . What's that? . . . Sure I got the number. I got it writ down right here—'

Skillimore stopped speaking very suddenly. Holden had moved up on him, picked up the pistol and wrenched the telephone cord out of the wall.

'Old man,' Holden said, 'you talk too much.' He thrust the muzzle of the gun into Skillimore's side. 'Can you give me one good reason why I shouldn't kill you?'

He saw now that he should have locked the car and pocketed the keys; it would have been the sensible thing to do. But he had had no suspicion of Skillimore; he had even taken a liking to the old bird. Now he marvelled that he could have allowed himself to be so easily taken in by the two-faced old bastard.

'What good would it do you to kill me?' Skillimore said. He sounded perfectly calm and not at all scared. Possibly he did not believe that Holden had any real intention of killing him.

'I might get some satisfaction from doing it,' Holden said. 'You really took me in with your soft talk. I thought you wanted to help.'

'I don't help law-breakers.'

'I'm not a law-breaker.'

'Tell that to the cops,' Skillimore said.

Holden saw that he was just wasting time talking to Skillimore when he ought to be getting away from there as fast as he could. He wondered whether to tie the old man up before leaving but there seemed to be no point in doing so; he had done all the damage he could do. He picked up the slip of paper with the car number written on it, screwed it up and dropped it in his pocket. With any luck Skillimore would not remember it correctly.

When he drove away Skillimore stood and watched him go; possibly he was trying to memorise the number. Holden wished he had never seen the old man; now there would be people looking for a green Ford. Damn!

He drove aimlessly. It was drawing on towards evening now but it was still not time to go to the Hornsby place. He glanced at the fuel-gauge and saw with dismay that the petrol was getting low; it would be a fine thing if he found himself stranded and unable to get to the rendezvous. It was essential to have the tank replenished without delay.

Therefore as soon as he came to a filling-station he drew in and bought some petrol. The man who served him was dressed in white overalls and a baseball cap. It was a small place and Holden was the only customer. He thought the man gave him and the car a curious look, but then he told himself that he was imagining things.

He paid with a twenty-dollar bill and the man said he would have to go and fetch change. Holden saw him go to what was probably the office and he could still see him through the window when he was inside. He saw the man pick up a telephone and speak into it, and he was facing the window as though keeping an eye on the green Ford. Holden did not care for the look of it; why would the man be making a telephone call instead of getting the change? Maybe he was talking to the police. But on the other hand he might simply be answering a call that had come through when he walked into the office.

Nevertheless, it worried Holden. He saw the man put the telephone down but even then he did not immediately come out with the change. Was he purposely spinning out time in order to keep his customer there? Holden decided to leave without the change; he got the car moving and was on his way when the man in the white overalls came out on to the forecourt, waving his arms and shouting. Holden could see him in the mirror but he did not stop. He wondered whether the man had taken his number. Nothing seemed to be going right.

He was feeling rather hungry now. Perhaps he ought to have accepted Skillimore's offer of ham and eggs but the old man's kitchen had sickened him. He toyed with the idea of going into Briggsville, parking the car and getting a meal somewhere. But he decided that it was too risky. He wondered where the motor-cycle riders had gone. If it had not been for them he could have spent the day peacefully enough in the bus; and he even thought about going back to the quarry to see if anyone had been there to investigate; if the place was deserted it would prove that the yobs had not gone to the police.

But he soon dismissed that idea also; it would be foolhardy to venture anywhere near that area now; it would simply be asking for more trouble, and he had about as much as he could handle already.

He felt a sense of relief when it began to grow dark, and after a while he found another place where he could take the car off the road a few miles out of Briggsville. It seemed to be an unofficial dump for old motor-vehicles and he drove the Ford in amongst them and switched off the lights. Here he felt he had the perfect camouflage and would be reasonably safe from detection. He settled himself as comfortably as he could and prepared to kill the time that still remained to be killed.

CHAPTER FIFTEEN

CAT-AND-MOUSE

It was getting on for half-past eight when he backed the car out of its hiding-place and headed towards the Hornsby Stud Ranch. He was allowing himself ample time and there was no need to hurry. He drove carefully; there was not much traffic on the minor road he was following and if it had not been for the nagging pain in his side and the thought of what might be lying in wait for him at the end of his journey he might have felt reasonably satisfied with the way things were going.

When he approached the gateway to the private road that led to the house he looked about for any sign of parked cars but he could see none. It worried him a little, for correct timing was going to be essential if matters were not to go badly wrong. So suppose the man who had spoken to him on the telephone had not believed a word he was saying, but had put him down as a crank or a hoaxer and had done nothing about it. What then? What then, indeed!

But no; that was not possible; they could not simply brush the matter aside like that; they would be bound to investigate. But would they? These were not British police he was dealing with; maybe they ordered things very differently in this part of the world. Here, so he had heard, there was a great deal of bribery and corruption, and perhaps Hornsby even had the lawmen on his pay-roll; perhaps he already knew all about the telephone call and had taken appropriate steps. But surely that was not possible, either; he refused to believe it. Nevertheless, that absence of any sign of a parked car was disquieting. He did not care for the look of it at all.

He turned in under the arch and drove down the approach road, with the white fences showing up in the glare of the headlights. And then he saw the house; the terrace illuminated by a diffused kind of light but completely deserted; the chairs empty, the tables bare; presenting, he thought, an oddly cold and unwelcoming appearance which made his spine tingle. For a brief moment he had an impulse to turn the car quickly and drive away from there; but it would have been a cowardly and a foolish thing to do, for it would have solved nothing.

When he had stopped the car he sat there for a while with his hands resting on the steering-wheel, not moving. No one had come out on to the terrace and he guessed that the black servants had been ordered to stay in their own quarters. He was wearing his gaberdine jacket with the zip-fastener and now he took the Walther pistol and slipped it into one of the pockets. He got out of the car, opened the boot and lifted out the biscuit-tin containing the bags of cocaine. From the direction of the stables he heard the faint sound of a horse moving in its stall; it was a still evening and apart from that there was almost complete silence, so that the noise he made closing the lid of the boot seemed very loud indeed.

He left the car and walked up to the terrace. He had just reached it when Marcia Brent came out of the house.

'So,' she said, 'you got here.'

'Yes, I got here.'

He noticed that her lips were swollen, no doubt as a result of the blow he had given her with his clenched fist the previous evening. She was giving him no big smile of welcome and he would have said she was hating his guts for what he had done; she would be pretty sore when she looked in a mirror and saw how much her good looks had been spoilt—if only temporarily. Well, if it came to the point, he was none too pleased with her, either; she had inflicted more serious damage on him than he had on her, even if it was not visible for all to see; and that damage was still giving him plenty of discomfort.

She looked at the tin. 'Is that it?'

'Yes.'

'Where did you have it hidden?'

'It was buried,' he said; and as he said it he thought of Gomez, who was to have been buried last night. He wondered whether they had got round to doing it after the business at the quarry. Perhaps, with Morton out of action, it had had to be postponed; perhaps Gomez was still down there in the cellar in his coffin.

'You lied, Ray. You said you didn't know where it was.'

'I didn't know, not for certain. They might have dug it up. But they were too smart; they didn't trust you; they meant to see the colour of your money first.'

'Not smart enough,' she said, with a little spurt of venom. 'They're dead, aren't they?'

'Yes, they're dead.'

'So it didn't help them much.'

'Look,' Holden said, 'I didn't come here to talk about that. It's done. Do we go inside?'

She turned abruptly and led the way into the house. Holden followed closely, the biscuit-tin under his right arm. It was like the fly walking into the spider's parlour and the big question was whether he would ever walk out again. The Hornsbys, uncle and niece, tended to have a rough way of dealing with people who crossed them. And he had certainly done that.

'In here,' Marcia said.

Hornsby was waiting for them. He was sitting in a comfortable armchair and he looked relaxed and untroubled, neatly dressed and as well-groomed as ever.

'Come in, come in,' he said. 'I am pleased to see you again, my boy. Sit down, won't you?'

He indicated a chair but Holden remained standing. He had seen at a glance that there was no one in the room besides Hornsby; no Morton, no Katz; above all, no Ruth Belding.

'I see you have brought the—ah—merchandise with you,' Hornsby said.

'I've brought it.'

'May we see it?'

'Where's Miss Belding?' Holden asked.

Hornsby smiled. 'Oh, I see what it is. You do not trust us. You think something evil may have befallen the young lady. It is not so, I assure you. Marcia, my dear, perhaps you will be good enough—'

Without a word Miss Brent turned and left the room. Holden was still standing. He felt tense and suspicious. He wondered where Katz was.

'You really should sit down, you know,' Hornsby said. 'It would be more restful.'

'I prefer to stand,' Holden said.

'As you wish.'

Marcia Brent came back with Ruth Belding, who cast a swift glance at Holden. She looked pale and nervous but was apparently unharmed. Holden was relieved to see her; until this moment he had not been certain that she was still alive.

'You're all right?' he asked.

She nodded but said nothing.

'Miss Belding has been well treated,' Hornsby said. 'You yourself should know that we are not unaware of our duties towards a guest. Now perhaps you will open the tin.'

There was a small table close to Hornsby's chair. Holden walked across, placed the biscuit-tin on the table and removed the lid. Then he stood back, watching Hornsby.

Hornsby took one of the polythene bags from the tin and gave it a cursory inspection, not even bothering to open it. Then he put it back in the tin.

'What a deal of bother would have been avoided if you and your friends had had the good sense to bring this straight to me instead of getting foolish ideas into your heads of making a lot of money for yourselves! You should have realised that was a very dangerous game to play.'

'We did realise it.'

'And yet you decided to take the risk. You were too greedy to let the chance slip by. It hasn't done you much good, has it? Your accomplices are dead and you, I believe, are injured.'

'I'm all right.'

'You don't look well. You should not have

202

struck my niece; that was an ungentlemanly thing to do. You can't blame her for shooting you.'

'I should have put a bullet in his damned heart,' Miss Brent said vindictively. She looked at Holden with hatred in her eyes.

'No, no, my dear,' Hornsby said; 'don't say that. If you had killed Mr Holden, who would have found the cocaine for us? We needed him. We do not need him any longer, of course, but—'

To Holden those last words sounded ominous. He said; 'I think it's time we were leaving. You've got what you wanted and there's nothing more to discuss.'

Rather to his surprise, Hornsby made no objection. 'Of course. You must forgive me if I do not feel bound to pay you the remainder of your fee. But then, I never got the car, did I?'

'The car was for Mr Bradley,' Holden said.

Hornsby chuckled. 'That's true. So perhaps you had better go to Mr Bradley for the money. Goodbye, Mr Holden. And goodbye to you, Miss Belding. I doubt whether we shall meet again.'

Marcia Brent accompanied them out of the house but she uttered no word of farewell. She remained standing in the doorway as they made their way to the car, watching them. There was in her manner, Holden thought, a curious expectancy; she seemed to be waiting for something to happen. He did not like it.

The green Ford was the only car standing in front of the house. The girl was slightly ahead of him as they walked towards it. He slipped his right hand into the pocket of his gaberdine jacket and grasped the butt of the pistol.

'Keep going,' he said. 'Get into the car.'

He turned then and looked back towards the house. Marcia Brent was still standing where they had left her; she had not moved. She was waiting for something; he knew it. But what?

And then he saw Katz step out of the shadows at the far end of the terrace on his left.

'Now where do you think you're going?' Katz said.

'We're leaving,' Holden said.

Katz came a little nearer. He was carrying the submachine-gun in his hands; it was just about on a level with his right hip and pointing at Holden.

'Not yet,' Katz said. 'And maybe never.'

Holden had turned to face him and out of the corner of his eye he could see that Ruth Belding was on the other side of the stationary car but was making no move to get into it.

'You were pretty damned clever last night,' Katz said. 'You gave me the slip. But not this time. No way, feller, no way.'

The woman standing in the doorway suddenly screamed at him: 'Kill the bastard! Kill him! What are you waiting for?'

'Patience,' Katz said. 'All in good time. Let him sweat a bit first.'

Holden could see that Katz was a connoisseur; he liked to savour his killing. He had hurried it at the old quarry but that was because there had been need for haste. Here he was not pushed for time and he was enjoying himself. But the end would be the same, because if Holden made one move to pull the Walther out of his pocket Katz would squeeze the trigger of the submachine-gun and it would be curtains for one. After which he would deal with the girl at his leisure; for there could be no doubt that she was on his list, too.

And still there were no cars on the approach road, no sign of anything. And if they had been coming at all they would surely have been there by now; so it looked as though they were not coming; he was on his own and he had only the small black pistol to get himself and the girl out of trouble. And the pistol was not enough.

'Are you sweating, punk?' Katz inquired.

'No,' Holden said. 'It's not that warm.'

'It's warm enough. You're sweating.'

He was right at that, dead right. Holden could feel the moisture in his armpits, in the palm of the hand that was gripping the gun. He was afraid.

'For Christ's sake,' the woman in the doorway screeched, 'finish it. Or do I have to get my own gun and do it for you?'

'No need for that,' Katz said. He shifted the submachine-gun slightly, as though bringing it into a more comfortable position.

He'll do it now, Holden thought. He's played his little game of cat-and-mouse and now he'll shoot, now he'll finish it.

But then Katz turned his head slightly, as though he had cocked his ear to catch some faint sound. And a moment later Holden had caught it, too—the sound of a car engine, and maybe more than one. He glanced towards the approach road and saw the glow of headlights. So maybe they had come at last. But they were late; too damned late.

He saw Katz's head move again and he hauled the Walther out of his pocket and fired it—once, twice, three times, in quick succession. Katz staggered and his legs began to fold but he still had a grip on the submachine-gun. Holden flung himself to his right and heard the gun stuttering. Something slammed into his chest and his leg and his arm, and he was falling. He thought he heard Ruth Belding cry out, and then the ground hit him, and everything was swimming round and there was nothing he could really hold on to any longer.

The cars were a lot nearer now and lights were flashing all over the place. And then he was vaguely aware of someone lifting his head and holding him and maybe crying a little, too; but it was all drifting away from him and there

206

was no way of getting a grip on it. Not any more; maybe never any more . . .

CHAPTER SIXTEEN

A Place to Live

The nurse said: 'You have a visitor, Mr Holden.'

'Oh,' he said.

The nurse was young and she was not at all bad to look at, if you liked them rather on the short side and black-haired and round-faced. She was, Holden thought, not altogether unlike Rosita Gonzalez, who had come to such a violent end in that old quarry; and he just hoped nothing like that would ever happen to this girl, because she was really very nice and seemed to enjoy doing things for him.

But the fact was that they had all been pretty good to him in the hospital—the doctors, the nurses, everybody. And he had certainly needed their help to keep him alive. One of the bullets from Katz's gun had gone very close to his right lung and another had smashed a rib; and what with those and the one in his leg and the other in his arm, not to mention the bit of damage that Marcia Brent had already done to him, it had been touch and go for quite a while, with his life teetering on a razor's edge, as it were.

But they had done everything that could possibly be done for him, and gradually they had pulled him back from the brink, until now there was no longer any danger of his passing prematurely away. Which was much to the satisfaction of all concerned, and that included a lot of people who were engaged in the business of seeing that the laws of the United States of America were not held in contempt.

For the fact was that they needed him; they needed him badly. He was to be the key witness when Mr Charles Hornsby and Miss Marcia Brent and a few other people, including a man named Katz and another man named Morton, came up for trial on various charges connected with the smuggling of narcotics, and murder, and a few lesser crimes.

In view of the fact that he had given certain information leading to the arrest of the aforesaid characters and had agreed to give evidence against them, he himself was not to be charged with any offence that he might have committed; and as soon as the trial had been completed he would be free to leave the country if he wished to do so.

Even without his evidence, of course, the case against Hornsby and the others would have been a fairly solid one, since a quantity of cocaine had been found in Hornsby's possession, as well as the body of a man named Gomez in a box in the basement of Hornsby's house; and Gomez had certainly not died from natural causes. Nevertheless, Hornsby would be bound to have some very smart lawyers defending him, and a witness like Holden would make the case for the prosecution just about as strong as it could possibly be.

So nothing had been too good for Holden in the way of medical attention. He had a private room in a top-class hospital and just about anything he cared to ask for; and he might have been more than a little worried about what it was all going to cost him, seeing that things like this were very expensive in Texas and did most certainly not come on the National Health. But fortunately that was all being taken care of and he had been assured that it would not cost him a cent; so he was able to relax and not bother his head with trying to work out how many years of his life he would have to labour in order to pay off the debt.

He asked there why they had not turned up a shade earlier on the night of the shoot-out at the Hornsby Stud Ranch; it would have saved him the unpleasantness of having four bullets inserted in his body.

'I might have been killed,' he said.

They said they were sorry about that but it had to be that way. 'We had to be sure the cocaine had been handed over. If we'd got there too early the whole operation would have been shot to pieces.'

'Oh,' he said, 'I see what a tragedy that would have been. Of course it was far better to have me shot to pieces than your operation.'

'You'll be okay,' they said.

Well, maybe. But if he had not put those three slugs into Katz he would certainly never have survived to give his evidence in the Hornsby trial. So he figured they owed him all he was getting; he surely did.

When his visitor came in he saw that it was Ruth Belding. He was glad they had not arrested her; she had not really played any part in the law-breaking and it would have been a travesty of justice if she had been shoved in gaol. He thought she was looking very lovely, and she made the hospital room seem ten times more attractive when she walked into it.

'Hello,' he said. 'It's a long time since I saw anyone as nice as you.'

'I was here yesterday,' she reminded him.

'That's what I mean. It's been a long time.'

She came to the bed and bent down and kissed him.

'That was nice, too,' Holden said. 'Why don't you and I get married sometime?'

'I'd like that,' she said.

'Of course I haven't got a job and only about twenty dollars in hard cash.'

'I would never dream of marrying a man for his money,' she said. 'It would be too sordid.'

'That's just as well. Have you got any?'

'About ten dollars.'

'A grand total of thirty dollars. Do you think it's enough for the down payment on a house?'

'I doubt it. But why do you want to buy a house?'

'Well, it's best for a married couple to have a place to live, isn't it?'

'But darling,' she said, 'we do have a place to live.'

'We do?'

'But of course. Surely you haven't forgotten Brunhilde.'

'Oh, my God!' Holden said. 'That jazzy old bus. Are you going to drive or am I?'

Chivers Large Print Direct

If you have enjoyed this Large Print book and would like to build up your own collection of Large Print books and have them delivered direct to your door, please contact **Chivers Large Print Direct**.

Chivers Large Print Direct offers you a full service:

✮ **Created to support your local library**

✮ **Delivery direct to your door**

✮ **Easy-to-read type and attractively bound**

✮ **The very best authors**

✮ **Special low prices**

For further details either call Customer Services on 01225 443400 or write to us at

Chivers Large Print Direct
FREEPOST (BA 1686/1)
Bath
BA1 3QZ